I0962615

THE GENE POLICE

Elliott Light

**bancroft
press**

Published by Bancroft Press ("Books that enlighten")
P.O. Box 65360, Baltimore, MD 21209
800-637-7377
bruceb@bancroftpress.com
www.bancroftpress.com

ISBN 978-1-61088-217-0 (cloth)
Cover Design: J.L. Herchenroeder
Interior Layout: Tracy Copes
Also visit www.smalltownmysteries.com for more information

To all those persecuted, harassed,
bullied, kicked around, and otherwise
treated unfairly because of the color of their
skin, the shape of their face, or the slant of
their eyes

PROLOGUE

I live with four cats on what was once a poor farm outside the small town of Lyle, Virginia. I share a small suite of offices with an attorney named Robbie Owens in a renovated townhouse on the north end of town and spend most of my days in my office managing the estate of Reilly Heartwood, a famous country singer and my biological father. He was a generous man who left me a lot of money, what was once a poor farm, a mansion on the edge of town, responsibility for four elderly people who once lived on the poor farm but currently live in the mansion, and a maze of tax problems stemming from his donations to charities that had lost their 501(c)(3) status.

Reilly Heartwood, who performed under the name of CC Hollinger, died without telling me what our relationship was. My mother, to hide the shame of being pregnant with me, had married a nice but formal man named William Harrington and told me that he was my father. William, who stuck me with the preposterous name, "J. Shepard Harrington," neither played with me nor taught me what sons are supposed to learn from their dads. I guess he was nice to my mother in an old school way, but he wasn't pleased when my mother took to calling me Shep. He traveled a lot, so I wasn't surprised when one morning he wasn't there for breakfast. After a few days, I asked my mother if he was coming back, and she just said, "no." We never spoke of him again.

I am an attorney with expertise in corporate and commercial matters and a smattering of civil law issues. My limited knowledge of criminal law was acquired when I was prosecuted by the federal government for criminal fraud and sentenced to prison. I served three years before the legal system finally acknowledged, albeit reluctantly, that I wasn't guilty.

The experience exposed a system designed to value conviction rates over truth—a system that regards sentences as final and irrevocable. For me, the most important lesson learned was that it's far easier for an innocent person to get into prison than out.

I was released from prison in time to watch my mother die of cancer. Less than a year later, I came to Lyle to deal with Reilly's untimely death from a gunshot wound initially reported as self-inflicted. I insisted that he wouldn't have killed himself and, in fact, proved that he'd been murdered. That's when I learned he was my father. While poking my nose into Reilly's death, I also learned what it was like to be shot. Having been shot once, you might think I wouldn't get involved in another murder investigation. But last summer, I was drawn into the murder of a woman who worked at a research facility that used chimpanzees as test subjects. Sydney Vail, who was later accused of the crime, brought me a stolen chimp named Kikora. Defending Sydney and Kikora was legally challenging, not to mention painful. I was shot for the second time, an experience that would make a rational lawyer think twice before getting involved in a third murder.

While not wanting to sound defensive, I did think twice—actually more than twice—about getting involved in the murder case of Jennifer Rice. I set boundaries to avoid being drawn in too deeply. I agreed to help around the edges of the case. My good intentions, however, were undone by an overdeveloped aversion to people who believe they can hurt others and get away with it. So while I denied that I was trying to find out who killed Jennifer Rice, I was wondering who did.

Jennifer Rice was in her late seventies when she was beaten to death. Although she was famous for her travel books and photographic essays, I had never heard of her until Reggie Mason appeared in my office to ask a favor. Reggie is a black state trooper whom I met while working the Sydney Vail case. He is a large, bear-like man in his early forties. To some, he appears intimidating, but he is one of the gentlest men I've ever known.

I hadn't seen Reggie Mason for several months when he arrived at my office on a cold February day in 2002. Perhaps his arrival alone should have alerted me to the import of his visit. Certainly I should have read the cues on his face to know that his visit wasn't personal. Any misconceptions were quickly dispelled when Reggie announced that he needed to confess to various crimes and wanted my advice on how he should proceed.

Reggie's announcement certainly defined his future. He told a simple story of what he did and why. Because his actions constituted crimes under Virginia statutes, his future was in the hands of the power brokers of the legal system: the police, a prosecutor, and a judge. He asked me, my law partner, and Robbie to help him decide when and how to admit to his wrongdoing.

Yet, his announcement actually told volumes about the past—a past that none of us knew anything about, and one that would soon appear one painful revelation at a time.

CHAPTER 1
Monday, February 11

The morning started innocently enough. Robbie was in her office talking to a client about a fence that had been installed on the client's property by the client's neighbor. I was working on a spreadsheet of Reilly's charitable deductions going back fifteen years in preparation for turning over Reilly's tax issues to a tax attorney.

My door was open, giving me a view of our small waiting room and the front door. My attention alternated from my computer screen to a large icicle hanging menacingly over the waiting room window. The icicle refracted the sunlight into a small swath of colors that flickered on the carpet. Objectively, this light display was not terribly exciting, but when compared to the unrelenting boredom of tax returns, the colors were fascinating.

The spell of the lights was broken when the door to the office was thrown open, allowing a surge of cold air to rush in. A moment later, the doorway was all but filled by the frame of Reggie Mason. He hesitated for a moment, then stepped inside and removed his dark glasses, his face expressionless while his eyes adjusted to the light. As I stood up, he saw me and flashed a smile.

"Hey, Shep. You got a minute?"

"What the hell are you doing here?" I offered him a hand, but he wrapped his arms around me and gave me a man-hug. When I stepped back I saw weariness and angst written on his face.

The door to Robbie's office opened and her client stepped out. The client was a small white woman, and she seemed to step back at the sight of a large black man. But he nodded his head, said "'ma'am" in a soft, southern voice, and she erupted in a smile. Reggie had that effect on people.

Robbie walked the client to the door and returned with a scowl on her face.

"It's good to see you, Reggie," she said firmly, "but I can't remember the arrival of an uninvited visitor, especially a cop, that wasn't made memorable by bad news."

Reggie shrugged. "Whether news is bad or good kind of depends on your perspective. I just need a favor."

"Why does the word 'just' always precede a request that smart people would say no to?" she asked.

Reggie forced another smile. "Maybe you'll say no. Maybe you won't."

"I'm sorry, Reggie, but men in general are untrustworthy. Cops and ex-felons even more so," Robbie said. "You've got a folder in your hand, so pardon me if I don't believe you're here to use the bathroom."

I am technically not an ex-felon. Robbie knows this but uses the reference when she's annoyed with me. From her tone, she suspected that Reggie and I were up to something that would distract me from my estate work. I decided it was best to allow her to negotiate with Reggie, but after two months of looking at tax records, I admit to being intrigued by what was in the folder he carried.

"All I want is a few minutes of your time," pressed Reggie. "After that, you can just say no. I hope you won't, but no hard feelings if you do."

Robbie led us into our small conference room. Pulling back a chair, she said, "You are going to explain why you're here, and then I'm going to explain how Shep has a meeting with an IRS agent in two weeks and can't be distracted until the audit is over."

Reggie took a seat. "It's just a small favor."

Robbie and I sat across from him. "What favor and how small?" she asked sternly.

Reggie opened the file and removed a stack of photographs. "Look at these and then I'll tell you what I need."

Robbie and I stared at a series of sweeping views of a pasture brimming with wild flowers. A farmhouse rose in the distance, a curl of smoke coming from its chimney. The photos were oddly familiar. A moment later, we stared at a close-up of the farmhouse that is now my current residence. The next picture stunned us both.

"Oh my God!" exclaimed Robbie. "That's Carrie! She can't be much older than we are now. She's so cute!"

In the next photo, two teenage boys with hardened, muscular bodies were leaning over a fence. "I think that's Harry and Cecil Drake," I said.

"No way," said Robbie excitedly. "Look at them. They're just kids."

I handed her a picture of a tall, thin man in his twenties standing on the porch and holding a cat. "That is Jamie Wren." Jamie Wren is now confined to a wheelchair and has trouble speaking.

The four of them—Carrie, Harry, Cecil, and Jamie—live in the mansion I inherited from Reilly Heartwood and are affectionately known as the "Residents." Cecil and Harry are now in their sixties, Jamie a little north or south of seventy, and Carrie over eighty.

We continued to shuffle through pictures of men and women that we didn't recognize. "Who took these and where did you get them?" asked Robbie.

"I don't know who took them," said Reggie. "But I thought you might ask the folks that used to live on your farm if they know. It would help me a lot."

"Help with what?" I asked.

"Just something I'm looking into," he said.

Robbie tossed the pictures onto the table. "That seems like a small enough favor, but there's no way we are going to help you look into something without knowing what it is. If this were official, you wouldn't be here. That may sound distrustful, but we need to protect our law licenses. Where were the pictures found and what are you looking into?"

Reggie looked at me. "Is she always like this?"

I nodded. "She is, but she's also right."

"I believe I'm guilty of illegal use of the state DNA databases and maybe a few more felonies. I'm trying to decide whether to turn myself in. Finding out who took the pictures of the poor farm might help."

I glanced at my friend, his usual happy demeanor replaced by a defiant gaze tinged with fear. Robbie looked at me, her distrustful attitude receding under the weight of Reggie's words.

"Give me a dollar," I said. Reggie returned a puzzled look. "We need to establish attorney client privilege."

Reggie handed me a ten. "I need that for lunch."

"Okay. Let's start at the beginning."

"Hold on," said Robbie. "We're not criminal attorneys. I don't know that we can provide you the kind of representation you need."

"I know that," replied Reggie. "But I trust you. That's the most important thing."

"Start by explaining why you were playing with DNA databases," I said.

Reggie hesitated, glanced at Robbie, then said, "It involves a murder."

I heard Robbie take a quick breath. "And you didn't mention this because…?"

"Because you might think I'm asking Shep to investigate the murder, and I'm not."

Robbie took Reggie's hand. "Now I'm completely lost. You want us to find someone who took photographs at the poor farm fifty years ago because that will help you solve a murder?"

Reggie shook his head. "No. Well, kind of maybe."

"One more time," I said, "and this time start at the beginning."

Reggie nodded and took a deep breath. "I was raised by my Aunt Betty after my parents were killed in a traffic accident. I was sixteen and she was forty-six. My Uncle Carl was in prison for armed robbery. Aunt Betty didn't have children, so she spoiled me a bit. When I entered the police academy, she told me that in 1953 she went to Sweetwater Hospital and gave birth to a baby boy named John Mason Langard. Sweetwater accepted black patients, so her race shouldn't have been a problem."

"But it was," offered Robbie.

"That's not it," replied Reggie. "Aunt Betty was told that the baby died of a heart defect, and that she had complications during childbirth that left her unable to have any more kids. Aunt Betty didn't believe the story they told her about Baby John and asked me to find out what really happened. To make her feel better, I said I would. I thought that would end it. But she kept asking me if I'd learned anything. I didn't have the courage to tell her that I had no idea how to investigate his death. I guess she thought that since I'd become a cop, I could just go into some file and look it up."

"What did she think happened to Baby John?" I asked.

"Either he was given away or he was murdered."

Robbie shook her head. "You don't believe that, do you?"

"I didn't at first," said Reggie, "but when you've heard the whole story, you can decide for yourself. So, Virginia was one of the first states to maintain a DNA database of felons. I became a trainer in the use of the database. I selected my uncle's DNA profile as a training tool. With each class, I ran his DNA against new samples entered into the database, hoping to find a partial match in the database that I could use to determine if Baby John was still alive.

"To be clear, the odds of this working were very small. The DNA used in criminal investigations is not particularly useful for establishing family connections. I had my aunt's DNA profile, so I had a pretty good idea of what my cousin's profile would look like. Even so, for me to find him, he would've had to have been at a crime scene in Virginia where DNA samples were taken, or he would've had to have been accused of committing a serious crime. I did this for ten years just so I could tell my aunt that I hadn't given up.

"And then last month, the system provided a sample that statistically had a high probability of being the offspring of my aunt and uncle. I didn't believe it would ever happen, but there it was. The sample was taken from the house of a murdered woman. The murder victim was an elderly white female named Jennifer Rice."

I was eager to learn more about the murder, but Robbie cut me off.

"Why would the hospital lie about your cousin dying?" asked Robbie.

"I don't know," replied Reggie. "But using the DNA database for personal reasons is a felony."

"I'm not sure if your conduct was actually criminal," I said. "I mean, you were authorized to access the database for training purposes. I don't see the point in telling anyone, particularly since you used the data you acquired for a legitimate purpose."

"The thing is, officially, my uncle had no children, so there is no reason for the investigators of Jennifer Rice's murder to look at DNA profiles in which some, but not all, of the loci match. I haven't told them about Baby John, so I'm probably obstructing a police investigation, which I suppose is another crime."

"What does any of this have to do with the pictures of the poor farm?" pressed Robbie.

Reggie handed us one more photo. Robbie and I studied it, unsure for a moment what we were looking at. The picture was back-lit. In the foreground, intentionally underexposed, was the silhouette of a woman. She appeared to be holding something against her chest.

Robbie took a sudden breath. "It's a baby!"

Reggie nodded. "That picture was taken at Shep's farm fifty years ago."

"You think it's your cousin?" I asked.

"Of course I do, but rationally it could be anyone's baby. It may be white or it may be black. I think the woman is white but I can't be sure. But it's all I have. If I can find the person who took the pictures, I might be able to find my nephew. In case I'm charged and arrested, I need to track him down before I confess to anything. I also need to know what he was doing at the scene of a murder."

"Okay," I said. "I get that you want to find who took the pictures and find your cousin. But let's talk about you confessing to what might be technical violations of the penal code. You know that's a bad idea."

Reggie leaned back in his chair. "I'm sure it is, but I'm kind of in a pickle."

"Explain pickle," said Robbie.

Reggie nodded. "The victim, Jennifer Rice, was seventy-eight when she was beaten to death in her home in Winchester. Detective Hunter

Darnel is in charge of the investigation. The evidence points to a handyman named Albert Loftus. The case against Albert looks solid. They found a few pieces of Ms. Rice's jewelry in Albert's truck. Albert's story is what you might expect. He said he came to the house to clear the gutters of ice. He knocked and went inside to hook up a hose to the hot water heater. The door wasn't locked, which he says wasn't unusual. When he called out, Jennifer didn't answer. He saw a dark liquid on the tile floor in the living room, and followed a blood trail to the bedroom, where he saw Ms. Rice lying on the bed. She was covered with blood and badly beaten. He said he panicked and ran out. He didn't call the cops because he says they don't like him. He's found Jesus and given up his bad ways. Despite the jewelry found in his truck, he says he didn't steal anything and never touched her."

"What put the police on to Albert in the first place?" I asked.

"An anonymous tip."

"A little convenient," said Robbie, "but he had her jewelry."

"He did," agreed Reggie, "but I'm not sure he killed her, and neither is Detective Darnel."

"Based on what?" asked Robbie.

Reggie shrugged. "It doesn't feel right"

"What do you mean?" I asked.

"At worst, Albert's a petty thief, but he's not violent. No one is considering any other possibilities because they have no reason to. If I come forward with what I've learned, Albert at least get's a fair shake."

"And you open yourself up to being prosecuted," I said. "But if Albert's guilty, then your concealing the information about Baby John would have no impact on the investigation and you would have confessed for no reason other than to clear your conscience."

Reggie nodded. "That's the 'if' I've been grappling with. I don't know what Detective Hunter would do with the information if I gave it to her. And if Albert's not guilty, then my cousin's DNA is certainly material to the case. He could be a person of interest. Of course, if I were to cause my missing cousin to be investigated for murder, my Aunt Betty would never speak to me again."

I pointed at the folder. "What else do you have?"

"Nothing you need to know about," replied Reggie. "Humor me."

Reggie opened the folder. "I don't have the full case file, but a friend of mine who logs in the evidence at the Winchester police department sent me these." He placed a stack of photos on the table. "These are photos of Germany after World War II that were found in Jennifer's house. We've determined that they were taken by a Seymour Van Dyke. They look to be original prints, so I'm guessing she knew him. I checked and he was pretty famous in those days. A lot of what he took was published in *Life Magazine* and in the major newspapers. The first few are pretty hard to look at."

Reggie placed another stack of pictures next to the first. "These are travel photos that the victim took."

Robbie and I flipped through a dozen pictures of concentration camp victims, orphaned children, and starving animals. The black and white photos were somber and reflective. The color photos were striking; in each, the central horror was framed by something normal – a flower, an aid worker's bright dress, a group of vigorous soldiers playing baseball. In one picture, a small boy sat on a pile of human bones holding a sign in German. When I showed it to Reggie, he grimaced.

"I'm told it says, 'Are my parents in here?' That's tough to get your head wrapped around."

A second group of pictures depicted harbors, beaches, streams flowing through forests, and ancient ruins. These, too, were framed with a flair for the artistic.

"Jennifer Rice took some very nice pictures," said Robbie.

Reggie nodded. "In the early fifties, she was modestly successful at selling stories about the war, mostly about the way refugees were treated. But when the public's interest in war journalism faded, she turned her attention to travel pieces and published a number of very successful guide books. The books were illustrated with pictures she'd taken of people and places she'd encountered on her travels. Her photos were published as coffee table books. The travel and photo books made her quite wealthy. But we're getting off track. The police don't care about photographs. I only care about the pictures taken at the poor farm."

I handed the photos back to Reggie. "Let me see if I have this straight. All you want us to do is to ask the Residents if they remember anyone taking pictures at the poor farm or if they saw a woman with a baby"

"That's all," replied Reggie.

"What if Jennifer Rice took the pictures of the poor farm?" asked Robbie. "What if she was the one with the baby?"

Reggie shook his head. "I don't know. I just need to understand why my cousin's DNA was found at the house where she died. Where that leads is anyone's guess."

We sat quietly for a moment.

"What a mess," said Robbie. She glanced at me, then at Reggie. "I think we can ask a few questions."

I can't explain why those words excited me, but I did my best not to show it.

With the favor asked and granted, Reggie stood up. "Thank you. Some police reports, the photographs, and a CD of scanned versions are in the folder."

"Promise me you won't speak with Detective Hunter or the prosecutor without speaking with us first," I said.

Reggie agreed and left.

Robbie was quiet for a few moments, her attention focused again on the pictures. She showed me the photo of the boy on the pile of bones. "Can you, for an instant, imagine what that was like? I can't. I can't imagine people doing this to other people." She shook her head. "You can't help but wonder why more wasn't done to stop it." She picked up the photograph of the woman with the baby. "Why would the hospital tell Reggie's aunt that her baby died if he didn't?"

"It's a mystery," I said.

"You don't think his cousin was actually murdered?"

I shrugged. "I have no reason to think so. If you're asking me if I believe that something like that might have happened, my answer is yes. The history we're taught was written by our parents and grandparents, all of whom were white. I doubt they were keen on sharing their generation's dirty laundry with their kids."

"Sounds like something you learned in prison," she said.

"Three years of mostly free time surrounded by some smart, educated inmates can open your eyes to the way the world is," I said.

Robbie grimaced, then tossed the pictures on the table. "I know you're worried about Reggie. But you can't get caught up in the murder of that woman. You just can't. I don't want you to, and none of your friends want you to. We can talk to the Residents about the pictures, see what they remember, and tell Reggie what we learn. I don't see how that can hurt anything, but that's all."

I smiled at her. "No," I said confidently. "That can't hurt."

CHAPTER 2
Monday, February 11

T he winter had started with a beautiful Christmas Eve snow putting everyone in a holiday spirit. Electric lights glowed under soft white flakes and town folk greeted each other with joy in their voices. But two months since then, snow and unending cold had become oppressive. Shoveling snow had become a chore that produced bad backs and short tempers. The sidewalks were layered with dirty slush balls and ice that made walking as dangerous as skydiving. A wide swath had been plowed down the center of Main Street, leaving room to drive but burying cars and parking spaces under mountains of dirty, frozen muck.

Heartwood House was only a half mile walk from my office, but with the wind and ice, and a pleading stare from Robbie, I elected to drive. Despite Heartwood House's numerous advantages, I chose to live on the poor farm while the former residents of the farm lived in the old mansion. I like living alone, probably a reaction to living with hundreds of other men for three years. And while the Residents are like family to me, I prefer to take them in small doses.

The house, with its deep red brick and dark blue slate roof, is stately under any conditions. Situated on a hill overlooking Lyle, the house offers a commanding view of the town to the south and the Blue Ridge Mountains to the north. And under a mantle of snow, the estate is postcard material. Add in a horse-drawn sleigh, and the scene would have been difficult for Currier and Ives to pass up.

As I stomped my boots on the front mat, the door opened. The four former residents of the poor farm, Cecil and Harry Drake, Jamie Wren, Carrie Toliver, and their housekeeper, Frieda, crowded into the foyer to greet me as if I were coming home from a lengthy absence, when in fact it had only been four days since my last visit. Their faces showed signs of boredom until they spotted Robbie.

"Don't dawdle with the door open," scolded Frieda.

Frieda Hahn had been Reilly Heartwood's housekeeper and, at my request, had stayed on to take care of the house and Residents. Getting used to her way of dealing with situations took some time. For instance, a scolding from Frieda is as likely to be a form of endearment as it is to be an indication of displeasure. Figuring out the meaning of a particular rebuke generally required some time and hindsight.

She approached Robbie with her warmer side. "Let me take your coat and get you something warm to drink, dear."

The Residents followed Robbie and Frieda into the kitchen, leaving me alone at the door.

Robbie and I have an ill-defined relationship. We met as children, explored the secrets of life in the poor farm barn, and went our separate ways. Circumstances conspired to bring us both back to Lyle—older and wiser, if not a bit broken. When I think of my happiest moments over the last six months, Robbie is a part of them. We look good together. We play nicely together. We work in the same office. The Residents love her and would like to see us paired up. And yet, there is no overt "we." Whatever the relationship is, we have adjusted to it.

With my boots off and my coat hung on a hook by the door, I made my way to the kitchen. Coffee was still brewing. The smell of bacon and biscuits wafted in the air. The six of us sat while Frieda cleaned a pan in the sink. Frieda often cleaned when she was angry, and I awaited a sigh and a commentary. I didn't wait long.

"I don't understand what you've done now, but I'm sure you've stuck your nose in something that's none of your business," she said without looking up. "Don't go denying it because we all heard about the policeman coming to your office. I guess we should be happy he didn't cuff you and throw you into the back of the car."

I heard Robbie chuckling, but she made no attempt to come to my defense.

"No one came to arrest me because I haven't done anything to be arrested for. What someone may have seen in our offices is not something we can discuss."

"For the love of God," snapped Frieda, "now you're going to get all wrapped up in another murder. Have you no common sense?"

"I think it would be fun," said Carrie. Carrie Toliver is petite but feisty. She believes she's over eighty, but she isn't absolutely sure. She is disarmingly charming, witty, and easily underestimated.

"I'm in," agreed Harry.

Cecil nodded. "Nothing better than a good mystery to cure cabin fever."

Harry and Cecil Drake are twins, probably in their mid-sixties, but without a record of their birth, it's impossible to be certain. Harry is outspoken while Cecil is often a man of few words. Both are experts with their hands. They can build or fix anything.

Jamie scribbled on a pad and handed it to Robbie. "When do we start?"

Jamie Wren, now confined to a wheel-chair, had come to the poor farm as an able-bodied man and, for unknown reasons, stayed. He had been labeled as "retarded," but my own assessment was that he was autistic. He lost the use of his legs and the ability to speak clearly because of a tick-borne illness. His disabilities produced behaviors that made him appear mentally slow. He spends most of his time in his room or in the sunroom scribbling fortune cookie fortunes and greeting card wisdom. He had recently turned toward Zenish aphorisms, finding commercial success with, "High expectations can ruin a new day."

As for Frieda, she often reaches pessimistic conclusions, then speaks about them as if they were proven facts. What she was asking for was assurance that her worst fears were without merit.

"It isn't like that," said Robbie, finally coming to my rescue. "We are not investigating a murder. We have been asked by a client to research photographs of the poor farm that were taken fifty years ago. Our client is eager to learn if anyone in town knows who took them. So the reason we are here is not about a murder, but to ask if anyone remembers someone at the poor farm who was taking pictures"

"So no one got killed?" asked Cecil.

"Well, someone did," replied Robbie, "but that's not important"

"Who got whacked?" asked Carrie.

"The victim's name is Jennifer Rice," I said. "She was in her late seventies. Someone beat her to death. But you're missing the point."

"You know better," said Frieda joining us at the table. She pointed a crooked finger at me and scowled. "Why does this always happen to you? You won't rest until you know who killed her." Before I could say anything, Frieda established the rules of engagement. "You circle the truth like a dog trying to lie down. Wears a body out hearing a lot of words that don't lead anywhere. If you're going to spin a tale, then don't bother saying anything at all."

"Rice was pretty old," said Harry. "Why would anyone kill an old person?"

"If they snored like you," said Cecil, "I'd say it was justifiable homicide."

Harry started to retaliate, but I cut him off. "You're missing the best part." One by one, I put the pictures on the table. The four Residents leaned forward, their gasps audible with each new image. When I was done, we spread the photos out across the table so all could be seen at once.

"That's you, Jamie!" exclaimed Carrie. "You could walk. I remember. Oh my God. Look at me!"

Carrie was easily recognized. The picture had captured her in her early thirties, roughly the same age as Robbie and me now. I couldn't imagine what it was like for her to spend fifty more years on the poor farm as her youth faded away.

"Who took the pictures?" asked Frieda.

"Lots of folks took pictures," said Carrie. "Ruth Littleton and her husband Philip took pictures all the time. They ran the farm. Sometimes they would invite people from the city to see what a poor farm looked like.

Some of those visitors took pictures too." She looked at a photograph of herself. "I don't know who took these."

"There was a woman with long blonde hair," said Cecil. "She was so pretty. She had this fancy camera. I saw it once, but I never saw her use it."

"A little skinny for my taste," said Harry, "but pretty."

Carrie laughed. "Harry had a crush on her. He was a teenager and had a crush on this woman who was close to thirty."

"I did not," he said, sulking.

Jamie scrawled a short note that Robbie read. "I saw her take my picture. Had to be before 1955 when I got sick."

"The blonde lady was pretty, and when she spoke to me, her voice was so soft," said Cecil. "I couldn't say anything back because Ruth said we couldn't. I think she thought I was mute or stupid."

"Well, she was at least half right," said Harry.

"Tell me about Ruth," I said before the twins could start bickering again.

Harry sorted through the photographs and handed me a picture of a plain but well dressed woman. "That's Ruth. She and her husband ran the farm in those days. The blonde lady was Ruth's friend. She stayed a few days in the main house. We weren't supposed to bother her."

"Did you ever hear her name?" asked Robbie.

"Nope," said Carrie, "and we knew better than to ask."

Frieda got up and checked the biscuits. "You'll have to clear the table if you want to eat," she said sternly.

Cecil stared at Harry. "Are you going to tell him?"

"You shut up," said Harry angrily.

"Harry once took her picture," said Cecil.

Harry dropped his gaze and, for a moment, I thought he might cry. Robbie took his hand and said, "That picture may help us find the woman who took the pictures at the poor farm. Do you know where it is?"

He shook his head. "I took it with Phillip's camera, but then he took the camera away from me. I never saw the picture."

"Okay," I said, "that's still good to know. We can look through the pictures at the farm and see if we can find it."

Harry's mood brightened. "She was with Dr. Adams. They were sitting on a hay bale by the barn. I don't think they saw me because I snuck up on them. You don't think she's the one who was murdered, do you?"

Harry hadn't known Ruth's friend except from a distance, and yet fifty years later, he still pined for this woman with long blonde hair. His question was so laden with loss that I struggled to answer. "I'm sorry, Harry. I have no idea. All our client asked us is to figure out who took the photographs at the poor farm."

"One more question," said Robbie. "Did any of you see the blonde woman with a baby?"

Carrie nodded. "She brought it with her when she came to visit. It had just been born, which is curious because she didn't look like someone who had just given birth."

"I didn't see the baby," said Cecil, "but I heard it crying a few times"

"I heard the blonde lady and Ruth arguing about the baby," said Harry.

"That made me sad because Ma and Pa used to argue about Cecil and me a lot before they got killed in the fire. Then we was given away to the orphanage. I wouldn't want to think about that baby going to an orphanage"

"The orphanage people were mean," added Cecil. "So we ran away and came to the poor farm. After we just started working, they fed us. That was good."

"We can eat the biscuits while they're hot, or I can throw them in the trash," said Frieda.

The pictures were cleared from the table to make room for coffee and biscuits. The subject of Phillip Littleton's camera was revisited. According to Carrie, the Littletons' took pictures to document how the poor farm was rehabilitating the poor folks who came there. "I was born on the farm and never left," she said, "so I guess my rehabilitation didn't work out so good."

Carrie wasn't actually born on the farm. At the age of four, she was dumped at the poor farm's entrance by relatives. She had invented the story of being born on the farm to avoid the pain of her abandonment, and only recently had shared her secret with me. If any of the other Residents knew the truth, they didn't let on.

I didn't want to upset Harry, but I forced the conversation back to the picture he'd taken. "So, do you think Doc knows who the photographer lady was?"

Harry shook his head. "Maybe. Doc only came out there that one day, so I don't think they was friends or anything like that. Of course, he was allowed to talk to her when we wasn't."

Harry's voice was tinged with jealousy.

"Maybe you should talk to Doc," offered Cecil.

Doc Adams was a caring man with a prickly exterior. He was not disposed to talk about the affairs of others. He was even less receptive to questions about his own life. Without the photograph, he would most likely dismiss the question outright. With the photograph, he would most likely respond with a tirade about minding my own business.

"Good idea, Cecil."

"I saw the baby on the porch just before the woman left," said Carrie. "Cute little boy. He was squirming around and then he looked at me. I don't think he could have smiled, but he got quiet. He grabbed my finger and tried to suck on it. That's when Miss Ruth came out and shooed me away. Until that day, I didn't know a white lady could have a brown baby, even a very light one. That was a surprise."

I had accepted Reggie's story about his missing cousin without actually thinking much about it. But with Carrie's revelation, the story had suddenly become more real and more tragic.

"The baby was brown?" asked Robbie.

"Oh yes. Like coffee with too much milk."

"So what happened to the woman and the baby?" asked Frieda.

I shrugged. "Who knows?"

"But don't you want to know?" snapped Frieda.

"I would," said Carrie.

"I'm in," said Harry.

"Agreed," said Cecil.

Jamie wrote a note and handed it to Robbie. "I have to know."

I waited for an objection from Robbie, but none was offered. It is, of course, easy to take the first step off a cliff when you don't know you're standing on its edge. Regrettably, after the reality of that first step is appreciated, it's too late to go back.

The Residents rushed off to search the Web for information about Jennifer Rice. Frieda left mumbling something about the laundry. Alone with Robbie, I stared into my coffee cup hoping to avoid a conversation I knew was coming.

"You're thinking," she said. "That's not usually a healthy thing for you"

"Nope. Just enjoying my coffee."

She leaned over. "Your cup is empty."

"So it is. Okay, so maybe I'm a little confused."

"Knowing that you're confused is a sign of increasing maturity," she said. "So, how can I help?"

"I get that what we've been asked to do does not include investigating Jennifer Rice's murder."

"That is true," said Robbie. "Of course, we have to protect Reggie from himself. He can't be asking questions."

"I could call Reggie and let him know what we learned and be done with it. But I've been asked to find out what happened to the woman that Harry saw with Doc and what happened to her baby. If Jennifer Rice is connected to the photographer, or if she took the pictures at the poor farm, then I may be involving myself in the murder investigation even though we just agreed I shouldn't."

Robbie gave me a dismissive look. "Sometimes you can be really annoying. You see things in black and white and miss the gray."

"Explain the gray to me," I said.

"It's like this. You kind of investigate, but not really. You ask a few questions, but not too many. And when you think you've investigated just enough, you tell Reggie you're done. That's the gray."

"Like a quasi-investigation."

"That's it exactly. No one is asking you to investigate a murder, particularly one the police think is solved. The police don't know about the baby, the woman who took the baby, or the photographer. So, as far as anyone outside this room is concerned, the questions you're going to ask have nothing to do with a murder at all."

"Okay. That clarifies things"

"So you're done thinking?"

"I think you've cured me of the practice. Thank you."

CHAPTER 3
Monday, February 11

I took Robbie back to the office and made up a story about needing to return to the farm to check on my cats. I promised to return in the afternoon.

The farm I inherited from Reilly had once been an institution modeled after the workhouses of England. A poor person received food and shelter in return for sweat labor. The original farmhouse was a modest stone building. A second story was added in the twenties, and bunkhouses were added during the Great Depression. Only one remained.

The kitties greeted me at the door and took turns trying to trip me as I walked. My cats are a motley collection of strays that have taken up residence at Heartwood House. I brought them to the farm when Heartwood House was being renovated to accommodate Jamie's wheel chair. A week after returning them to their original home, all four arrived at the farm hungry but no worse for their travels.

Rocky, a twenty pound Siamese, is the leader. Second in line is Van Gogh, a medium sized gray tabby, who is missing part of an ear. The local vet surmised that someone removed it with a knife. And while Van Gogh likes to complain about his deformity, he is remarkably trusting of humans. The smallest of the four is Molly, a small black and white kitty who purrs a lot and looks at me through squinted eyes when she wants to be picked up. Last is the irrepressible trouble-maker Atisha, a female orange tabby apparently named after a Buddhist master and scholar before her true nature had been revealed as a kitten.

I cleaned their food bowls and filled them with fresh canned food.

With starvation of the farm's feline residents prevented, I made a cup of hot cider and headed to the attic. What I found were half a dozen unmarked boxes, any one of which could have held the photograph. I set up a table in a downstairs guest bedroom and brought the boxes down from the attic. I waded through stacks of administrative records and found two albums of black and white photos. The albums looked to have been made from pages of black construction paper, now brittle, mottled, and bound together with a shoelace.

The pictures of Harry, Cecil, Carrie, and Jamie brought back lots of memories of summer days riding horses and driving an old Ford tractor. While the photographs were interesting, I couldn't find the picture that Harry had described.

I was certain there was another box of records, photographs, and stories that had been assembled by Terry McAdams, the last administrator of the farm when it was still operating as an institution for the homeless and destitute. Terry had been writing a history of the farm for nearly a decade but couldn't find anyone to publish it.

After searching the closets and hutches for the box, I reluctantly headed for the cellar. I found a flashlight with fresh batteries. As a kid, I'd been told that residents of the poor farm had been tortured in the dark cavern beneath the main farm house and that the ghosts of the victims still inhabited its damp and gloomy environs.

I flipped the switch at the top of the stairs and descended slowly. The basement extended the full width and length of the house. A single light bulb dangled from a wire in the middle of the abyss and cast a small globe of light that seemed unable to penetrate more than a few feet. An antique coal-burning boiler sat in the middle of the rectangular space, its pipes and valves extending outward like arms from a subterranean monster.

Next to it was a slightly younger, but functional, oil furnace. I was startled when the oil furnace rumbled to life, its metal duct work creaking against the sudden influx of hot air. A heavy bouquet of petroleum joined the smell of mildew and earth. It gave me another reason to keep my visit as short as possible.

I used the flashlight to scan the room from the perceived safety of the last stair tread. The walls were stone, held together by ancient mortar. The floor was dirt, but the well-trodden Virginia clay may as well have been concrete. Old bed parts and furniture lined the basement walls that ran under the front of the house. Shelves lined the back wall. I imagined the shelves full of wild strawberry and blackberry jam that the residents made in the early summer. Not seeing a shackled corpse, a rat, or a snake, I stepped carefully toward the center of the room.

I stand about six foot four. The space between the dirt floor and the lowest joists was less than six feet. I hunched over around the furnace and the old boiler while walking and scanning the wall with my light. I had hoped to find Terry's box and make a quick retreat. After two passes, I was satisfied that the box wasn't there, yet I wasn't inclined to leave.

My attention shifted to the wooden beams that ran from the front wall of the house to the back wall. These were massive timbers, probably oak at least eight inches wide and more than a foot tall. To my eye, it appeared that the beams toward the back of the house were sagging. The deviation was most noticeable right under the kitchen.

I inspected the back wall and found a small crack that ran almost the length of the foundation about four inches from the floor. Water had seeped through the wound, turning the clay below it the color of dried blood. I couldn't determine whether the crack was new or just old damage that had gone unnoticed, but the water seepage was new and worrisome.

My inspection was interrupted by the ringing of my house phone. I ran upstairs and managed to pick it up before it went to voicemail.

"You sound like you've been running, or perhaps I interrupted a hot date," said Robbie.

"I was in the basement looking for Terry's old papers."

"That's funny because they're in your office where I put them"

"You have Terry's papers?"

"I do. Last fall, I was looking for some information about Reilly's purchase of the poor farm. I would be happy to bring the box to you in exchange for a late lunch."

"I guess I could throw something together."

"I think I'll order Chinese. Given that this is a house call, I'll charge it to your account."

I hung up the phone and set the kitchen table. Thirty minutes later, I heard Robbie's car and met her at the porch. She carried a large box inside and placed it on the table in the guest room. While I was eager to see if the missing photo was in the box, I was drawn to the smell of Kung Pao Chicken from Brown's Chinese and American Restaurant. We ate in a comfortable silence, sharing smiles of satisfaction. The relaxed atmosphere came to an abrupt end when Robbie took a long slow breath and said, "We need to talk."

The words "we need to talk" when uttered by a female are powerful cues that a male should not take lightly.

"Whatever you think I've done, I didn't mean to do it," I said cautiously. "And of course, I'm extremely sorry and will never do it again."

"It doesn't matter whether you meant it or not. But, for once this isn't about you doing something stupid. It's about Eric."

"Eric? And who is Eric?"

"Who he is is not important. He called and asked if I wanted to go scuba diving with him in Belize."

"Really? Belize? So is there a question?"

"No. I just wanted you to know that I may be taking some time off."

I forced a laugh. "I'm a bit hurt that I wasn't invited." Robbie's cold stare indicated that my attempt at humor was not well received. "Okay. It's none of my business. If you want to go, you should go."

Robbie nodded. "Good."

"So, do you want to go?" I asked.

"I don't know. I'm sorry I mentioned it. Besides, as you said, it's really none of your business what I do. So, can we drop it?"

"Come on, Robbie. I don't know what you want me to say."

She took my hand. "I'm sorry. I know how things are with us. Sometimes, I wish they were different."

"How are things?"

"I love you dearly," she said, "but I'm not in love with you, however tempting you make it. This may sound cruel, but we're just too damaged for either of us to think we fit together. The good times are great, but sometimes you fall into a darkness that threatens to swallow you up. I went through that with my dad. I'm not going to go through it with you. We may have our moments, but there's no future in it. I need to know that you're good with that. I don't want to hurt you, and I don't want to be hurt either."

A silence ensued, which prompted another comment from Robbie. "Please don't sulk."

"Why is it that women brood and are viewed sympathetically, but men sulk and are derided for it?"

"The very fact that you don't know the answer means you wouldn't understand the answer if I chose to provide it to you."

I stared into her eyes. "You're right. But here's the thing. There are only a handful of people I care about and trust. You're one of them. I know I'm damaged goods. I get angry and sad. Sometimes, I drink too much. You can't fix me, and I don't want you to try. So, I think we're saying the same thing. But don't think for a moment that I take you for granted. That will never happen. Part of me doesn't want to hear about Eric, but most of me wants you to be happy."

The kiss was sudden, soft, and slow. Robbie pulled away, resting her forehead on mine, her breathing rapid and wanting. "God, sometimes being around you is like walking into a pastry store when I'm on a diet." She lingered for a moment, then said, "Let's just look at photos."

We cleared the table and went into the guest room where I had deposited the box.

"You could afford to fix this place up, you know."

Robbie was referring to the aging wallpaper and furniture I had inherited and still used. She was right, of course. My father, Reilly Heartwood, was a world-famous country singer. He left me more than twenty-five million dollars in assets and a continuous stream of royalty payments from his recordings. Prison took away my ability to support myself. Reilly's money took away the need to support myself. I have yet to master spending money that I didn't earn. So inheriting Reilly's money has left me in limbo—between the social order I knew in prison in which personal decisions were made for me, and the social order of the outside world in which one must make dozens of decisions every day. The house remains as I received it and, like me, stuck in a time warp waiting for something to change.

"This spring for sure," I said. "Now, focusing on the task at hand, we're looking for a picture of Doc by the barn with a woman with long blonde hair."

We divided the contents of the box into two piles and each sorted through one of them. Despite having pointed out that we were looking for a particular photo, Robbie was constantly asking questions about who was who and what each person was doing. I sat next to her and we went through the pictures together. A half hour later, I tossed a picture into the box that Robbie quickly retrieved.

"Did you look at this? That's us. Aw, we're holding hands."

I examined the picture closely. "You've got straw in your hair"

"I can't imagine why," she said.

Twenty minutes later, Robbie pushed a photo in front of me. Doc Adams was pointing his finger at the woman with long hair. She was, as Harry had said, quite pretty, despite a face etched with sadness. Whatever Doc was telling her was not what she wanted to hear.

"What do we do now?" asked Robbie.

I sighed. "As much as I would prefer not to, we need to ask Doc about the woman in the picture."

"He isn't going to like it. He's still angry with you for hunting down Reilly's killer."

"I know. But right now he's the only lead we have." I put the rest of the photos back into the box. "It's league night and beer is half price. I'm sure we'll find him at the bowling alley. Maybe if he's had a few, he'll be civil."

————————————————

When we arrived at the Bowlarama, we found the parking lot to be plowed and sanded and the sidewalk to the front entrance scraped to bare concrete. It's nice to visit a place where the priorities are firmly established.

As the owner of the Bowlarama (another bequest from Reilly Heartwood), I have certain privileges, the most important being that I don't pay for food. Apparently, that privilege extends to anyone in proximity to me when they order. Robbie ordered burgers and beers without offering to pay, then took a seat at an empty table.

Before I could search for Doc Adams, I felt a presence behind me. The presence revealed itself to be Sarah Mosby, Reilly Heartwood's older sister and my aunt. In her seventies, Sarah had long ago lost patience with the human animal, especially males. If she has an opinion, she expresses it. Otherwise, she isn't one for idle chatter.

She sat down, grabbed my beer, and took a long drink. "Hey, Robbie." Chester arrived with two orders of burger and fries. He placed one in front of Robbie. But as Chester lowered the second plate toward the table, Sarah followed it with her eyes.

Chester looked at me, and I nodded. "I'll have turkey on whole wheat," I said, "and another beer." He placed the plate in front of Sarah and walked away.

"I'm supposed to tell you that Doc is waiting in the office behind the bar," said Sarah. "He knows you've got a bone to pick with him. He's none too happy about it, but then it doesn't take much these days to set him off." Sarah laughed. "Getting old will do that to you. Course, I'd have thought Doc would be used to being old by now."

Robbie and I slipped behind the bar and opened the office door. Doc was seated on a sofa opposite an ancient desk. Mounted on the wall above the desk was a deer head, a stuffed owl, and a large mouth bass. The room smelled of tobacco and beer, and for a moment I thought Robbie was going to gag.

Doc glanced up at us through sad, fightless eyes, then fixed his gaze on the floor. "Frieda told me what you're up to, so no need to give me a history lesson."

I had anticipated a verbal brawl with Doc and found his demeanor worrisome. I handed him the picture that Harry had taken. Doc studied it, his index finger rubbing his lips as the image stirred old memories.

"Do you know her name?" I asked.

He shook his head. "I never heard Ruth call her by her name, and the woman never offered it. Do you think she was the woman who was murdered?"

The question seemed odd, apparently prompted more by guilt than logic.

"We don't know. We have no reason to think so."

"The woman who was killed. Was there a record of her having any children?"

I shook my head. "No. But we don't have the police file. We aren't actually involved in investigating the victim or the person who killed her. Our only interest is in finding out who the woman was and how she had a baby that wasn't hers."

Robbie knelt in front of Doc, her hands on his knees. "What is it, Doc? What's wrong?"

When Doc lifted his head, his eyes were flooded with tears. I have experienced heart wrenching moments, but the grief on Doc's face at that moment almost undid me.

"I could have helped her," he said. "She asked me to examine the baby to make sure he was healthy and to teach her how to take care of him. She wanted to save it from a future in the welfare system that she and Ruth understood better than me. She loved that baby, but I called the police. I did the right thing according to the law, when I should have done the right thing for that child. A day doesn't go by when I don't wonder about them."

I pulled up two chairs and offered one to Robbie. "Where did she get the baby?"

"How the hell should I know?" he snapped. "She and Ruth promised me they tried to reunite the baby and the birth mother. They explained again and again what would happen to a colored child in a social welfare system operated to help white babies. The woman in the photo pleaded with me to help her, but I was too mule-headed to listen. I called the authorities and the woman made a run for it."

The story Doc related was compelling but not terribly helpful. Without a name, we'd reached a dead end. Doc apparently sensed my disappointment.

"I didn't help her, and I can't help you," he said, "so can I go?"

I looked at the photo of the nameless woman, then at Doc. "What happened to Ruth?"

"She was angry and let me know it," replied Doc. "The cops came and she denied everything. She told them that some of the people staying at the farm had mental problems, and that I was most likely told a tall tale that only a city boy would believe. The investigator took a look at the poor folks on the farm and decided it wasn't worth the effort to ask any questions. About a month later, Ruth had a stroke that left her with mental problems. She was admitted to Lady of Comfort nursing home. I heard that she lived another ten years or so, but we never spoke again."

Doc shook his head and waved his hand as if engaged in an internal conversation. After a moment, he looked at me with pleading eyes. "I was a son-of-a-bitch back then. I know I've been hard on you about meddling in things that are none of your business. But I'm asking you to do whatever you can to find out what happened to that woman and child. Just don't go getting shot."

Doc pulled himself from the couch and seemed about to leave when I stopped him. "One last thing: Is there anyone still alive who might have known Ruth at the nursing home? Someone Ruth might have talked to?"

"She had a caretaker who looked after her from the day she arrived at Lady of Comfort until she died. Ruth Littleton's daughter might know. Last I heard, she was still alive. You understand she may not want to talk to me dead or alive." He stopped at the doorway, and said, "Good or bad, I want to know."

"Sure, Doc."

He shuffled out of the office, leaving me alone with Robbie. "I don't ever remember seeing Doc like that," she said.

"Maybe we should let this go," I said. "We're just stirring up a lot of old feelings, and I don't see it leading anywhere."

"I know you're just saying that for my benefit, but it's too late for that. I want to know. Doc wants to know. Everyone at Heartwood House wants to know. You want to know."

As I drove back to the farm, I tried to imagine the events that had unfolded there a half century earlier. How many lives had been touched by the arrival of the woman with a camera and a baby? Even today, Harry's broken heart had not fully healed, and the usually stoic Doc Adams was still riddled with guilt because of a decision that, under the circumstances, was both rational and justified.

I fed the kitties and tried to watch a movie. I lost track of the plot and turned it off. It was almost eleven when I decided to call Gus Jaynes. Gus is a former FBI agent whose testimony helped send me to jail. Later, he identified the witnesses who had lied at my trial and brought the matter to the attention of the court. I was released, but Gus was kicked out of the Bureau. The institutions of justice are seemingly fond of one-way doors. They don't like admitting to a mistake and don't suffer those who believe that the truth should set you free. Gus now runs a private investigation firm in Washington, D.C.

The phone rang twice before I heard Gus' voice. "Tell me you're not shot or arrested and I'll go back to bed."

"Not yet, but if you hang up, that could change"

"So who was murdered and why do you care?"

I gave Gus a summary of what I knew of Jennifer's murder and how I was connected to it. When I was explaining the part about the baby, Gus cut me off.

"It's late and I'm sleeping off a few too many scotches, so why don't you tell me what you want from me, and then we can talk in more detail in the morning."

"I want you to find out what you can about Jennifer Rice. She wrote travel books and was pretty good with a camera. I don't think it's a coincidence that a woman shows up at the poor farm and takes pictures. So, it's possible that Jennifer was the woman with the baby. If that's true, then maybe the baby is connected to her murder. I would also like information about a World War II photographer named Seymour Van Dyke. Jennifer had some of his photos in her house. I don't think there's any connection between the Van Dyke photos and the murder, but we might as well see if there's a personal connection between Rice and Van Dyke. I guess that's it."

"Are you sure you want to chase another rabbit down a hole?"

"I'm no expert, but I doubt that many house burglars are prone to beating old women to death. Reggie's in trouble, and there's the question about the black baby. Yeah, I'm sure."

CHAPTER 4
Tuesday, February 12

The sky was still dark when I tossed the photographs and a snow shovel into my car and headed out. I listened to an all-news station to get a traffic report. The good news was that the traffic was lighter than normal. The bad news was that the lighter traffic was due to the threat of heavy afternoon snow and high winds. Reports followed of snow plows readying themselves for battle and young meteorologists holding rulers to measure the snow as it fell. Twenty minutes of this hype and it became clear that anyone listening to the news in a car was doomed to die alone and cold.

Instead, I switched off the news and inserted a soft jazz CD. I was soon bathed in the sweet, mournful voice of a tenor sax, the deep percussion of a stand-up bass, and the subtle sizzle of a drummer working a drum set with wire brushes. Thirty minutes later, the sun rose over the snow-covered hills of the Virginia piedmont, tingeing them with a soft orange hue. At one summit, the saxophone wailed a chorus of "Wonderful World."

With most of the commuters scared away, the trip into DC took less than three hours. I arrived at Gus' offices just east of Dupont Circle a few minutes after ten and was directed to a conference room. Gus was seated across a table from a tall, pencil-thin man. Even from the back, I was certain he was talking to Zak Tully. Zak is a geek with a major in technology and a minor in forensics. He apparently graduated from high school without actually attending a majority of his classes. Zak claims he avoided school because people thought he looked like someone from a horror movie cast. (He does.) But it's his voice that grates on you. Talking in a raspy staccato, he seems to snort his words more than speak them.

Zak smiled when I walked in but didn't let go of a bagel thick with cream cheese and a thick slab of salmon. "Morning," he said, propelling a blob of cheese half way across the table.

"Morning," I said, taking a seat next to Gus and noting that Zak made no effort to remove the white projectile from the table's surface.

"I've briefed Zak on what you told me," said Gus. "We've started a background check on Jennifer Rice but haven't made a lot of progress. I'm sorry, but you may have made the long drive for nothing."

"I needed to bring you the file that Reggie gave me," I said, "and that was a good excuse to get out of Lyle."

I placed the folder containing the photographs and the CD on the table. Zak reached across and grabbed both. He flipped through the photographs in the file while making audible noises that alternated between groaning and cooing. After a few minutes, he grabbed another bagel and propped his feet on the table. "I can't tell you who took these pictures," he said.

The accurate reply was that I hadn't asked him to and didn't expect him to. But neither Gus nor I budged. Zak's body language indicated he had something to say about the photographs. Whatever he was thinking, he would share it in his own good time.

"It can't be done," I said, my tone equally hopeless. "I'm sorry I asked." I hadn't actually asked, but I saw no point in saying so.

He dropped his feet and snapped forward. "Three sets of photographs. Two of the photographers are women. Are the women photographers the same person? That's the question you should have asked Gus. Some would say it's impossible to tell, but I say the answer can be found if you know where to look."

"And you know where to look," said Gus in a patronizing tone.

Zak leaned across the table and whispered, "Were the pictures of the poor farm and the travel pictures taken with the same camera?" He raised an eyebrow as if the answer to the question was obvious.

I was about to say something patronizing when I realized Zak was right.

"One camera, one photographer, two names," said Zak. "That's what I'm going to find out."

Zak gave us a detailed explanation of how he intended to compare digitized versions of the pictures to see if they shared a unique camera aberration. The explanation included a list of the number of variables that had to be eliminated and the odds of success. Gus and I let him ramble for a few minutes about mirror scratches and dust and lens aberrations but stopped him when he described how he would use a computer in FBI headquarters to run the analysis.

"I think we will rely on your judgment as to how to proceed," said Gus, cutting him off gently. "Go ahead and brief Shep on what you've learned about Jennifer Rice."

Zak nodded. "I snooped around some of the government databases. Would it surprise you that Jennifer Rice was issued a social security card in 1953? Curiously, I couldn't find a social security number or tax records for Seymour Van Dyke at all."

"That's not unusual given the way birth records were often lost or destroyed," said Gus. "But it could mean something."

Zak grunted. "Maybe that's because before 1953 there was no Jennifer Rice. I'd like to know who she was before 1953. I'd also like to see the crime scene evidence and the autopsy report."

"Keep in mind," I said directly to Zak, "that I'm not investigating Jennifer Rice's murder."

Zak smirked back at me. "Of course you're not. That's why you drove three hours to get here."

"One last thing," said Gus. "I talked to Shaun Wiley, who works at the Library of Congress. He's an expert on the Library's photographic collection from the war years. They have records of photographers hired by the government to document World War II, and he's willing to help you research Seymour Van Dyke if you drop by." Gus handed me a slip of paper with Shaun's phone number. "Keep in mind, experts like him like to talk, so you have to keep him focused or you'll be there all day."

Gus had a copy made of the file and the CD, and he promised he'd call me as soon as he learned anything useful.

I stood in front of my car in the parking garage contemplating a drive back to my farm in a snow storm. If I left for home, I could beat the weather. But the Library of Congress was only a few subway stops away. I could still head back to Lyle before noon if I stayed focused. I called Shaun Wiley. I reached him walking to Union Station to catch a train home. He agreed to meet me at Starbucks if I could be there quickly.

The sun was a dull orb behind thin gray clouds as I took the escalator down to the Dupont Circle Metro station. Fifteen minutes later, I was pushing through a throng of people at Union Station. Starbucks was not crowded and I had no problem spotting a mousey white-haired man sitting at a table scanning the crowd. I was about to introduce myself when I heard someone calling my name. I turned to face a large, linebacker-sized man carrying a copy of *Rolling Stone* magazine. "He looks like a librarian," said the man, "but I am one. Shaun Wiley."

I ordered coffees and sat across from Shaun in a leather lounger. "World War II photography is one of my favorite subjects," he said, "but with the storm coming, I don't have much time. During the Depression, the Works Progress Administration funded photography projects. When the WPA disbanded in 1943, some of these photographers went on to cover the war. I found an Army pass issued for Seymour Van Dyke. I also found a set of photographs that were taken by him that included locations and people photographed by another photographer, Luci Turnbull. Luci worked with Seymour and can tell you more about him."

He handed me a print-out of a map, directions to a deli, and the ingredients for a sandwich. "After the war, Luci travelled all around Europe for both the government and for a news syndicate. She then became a psychiatrist. She's ninety-five but still active. I called and she said her art class had been canceled. She's expecting you for lunch in about an hour and instructed me on what she wanted you to bring. The address of her favorite deli and her selection is on the paper I gave you. Have the sandwich made just as I've indicated, or she will be pissed."

Before I could thank him, he stood up, wished me luck, and disappeared into the chaos of the station.

I took a few sips of coffee, then tossed it into the trash. I had asked about Seymour out of curiosity. I wish I hadn't. Now I was committed to provide lunch to Luci Turnbull, further delaying my escape from the city. The subway trains were packed. Automobile traffic, however, was still light. In thirty minutes, I was on Massachusetts Avenue heading north. Just beyond American University, I found the deli and had them make two sandwiches to Luci Turnbull's specifications. I turned onto Upton Street and pulled in front of a well-kept brick home. I checked the address, then stepped out into a cold wind and walked toward the front door. It opened before I'd reached the front stoop. A tall woman with a thick crop of white hair looked at me, then at her watch.

"You may have some good qualities, Mr. Harrington," she said sternly, "but promptness isn't one of them."

I hesitated, stunned less by the rebuke than the woman who delivered it. Luci Turnbull was old enough to have known Freud and seemed crusty enough to have been the cause of his cocaine habit. But she may have also frightened Father Time into leaving her with the stature and shape of a much younger woman. As she read my face, a smile danced at the corners of her mouth.

"Well, come in before you freeze," she said, waving me inside.

The foyer was decorated in a style that could politely be referred to as eclectic. To my eye, it looked like Luci collected junk without theme or sense of quality. Clay figures of gargoyles shared shelf space with porcelain angels. A pastoral scene was hung near an angry cubic rendition of a man with one eye.

I followed her into a small room where a table was set for lunch. At the back of the room, two easy chairs faced a stone fireplace that illuminated the room with a warm, flickering orange light. Tall windows flanking the fireplace offered a view of evergreen trees laden with snow.

Luci took the bag of food from my hand and set a sandwich on each plate. "This is where I treated my patients and they tested mine. The worst times were in the fall and winter, when darkness came early and hope was more fragile. For fifty years, I learned about the weaknesses of the human machine and the tendency of people to use misfortune as an excuse for laziness. I found that too much empathy only fed the victim complex. Toward the end, I met whining with a verbal assault that seemed more likely to cause a neurosis than cure one. I told them that if you're just coming to see me because you're tired of sulking by yourself, don't bother. I quit practicing before anyone committed suicide, but by then I didn't care one way or the other."

I started to offer to help with lunch, but Luci wasn't done. "I've read about you. I'd say you have whining rights for all the crap you've lived through, even if some of it was your own fault. So I'm going to give you some advice for free and then we can eat. Life is a struggle between those with power and those without. Power is relative. Sometimes you have it. Sometimes you don't. Little people never have it. Get over it."

"That's comforting," I said. "I could get that advice from the Eagles for fifteen bucks."

Luci's laugh filled the room. "I listen to the Hell Freezes Over CD in my Zumba class. You've got to love Don Henley's honesty. I hope lemonade is okay. I make it myself. Can't stand the crap they sell in the store. It actually goes well with the sandwich."

We ate without conversation. Luci made a comment about "too much mayo," followed by "there's always too much mayo." When she was done eating, she simply said, "Thank you."

I offered to clear the table but she declined. She took her drink and slowly dropped into one of the recliners in front of the fireplace. I followed. A log broke into pieces, which sent sparks flying up the chimney. "I get sleepy after I eat so you better ask your questions while I'm still interested. But first, if you would stoke the fire, I would be greatly appreciative."

I added two logs to the fire and closed the glass doors. "I'm looking into the murder of a woman in her mid-seventies," I said, sitting in the chair next to her.

"Murder is such a gruesome part of human nature. It's worse when it involves children."

For a moment, I wondered if Luci had misheard me. When I turned and faced her, she was gloating with joy at how easily she had befuddled me.

"Yes. Much worse," I replied. "Photographs taken at the poor farm where I now reside were found in the victim's home. We have no idea who took those pictures. But the victim had pictures taken by Seymour Van Dyke. I'm trying to establish if the victim had a relationship with Van Dyke. You were a war photographer, so I thought you might have known one or both of them."

I heard Luci sigh. "Almost sixty years ago. Where does the time go?" She sat motionless as she stared into the fire. I imagined that she was seeing memories stirred up by my request and wondering which ones to share with me. After a moment, she said, "The war was a heady time for women. We were learning to do jobs that men had done. We built airplanes, we ran factories, and we became reporters. Getting to cover the war wasn't easy, but by the time it ended, over a hundred of us had secured official military accreditation as war correspondents. Getting to the front was tricky, but not if you were creative."

Luci's gaze moved to the window to the right of the fireplace. "It's snowing. You need to leave."

The snow was light but steady. "Just a few more questions. Seymour's photos were found in the victim's home. I'm just wondering if you can tell me what happened to him."

Luci turned and looked at me with a mixture of incredulity and amusement. A moment later, she was consumed by laughter. She tried several times to stop, but each time she looked at me, she started laughing again. I was amused that she was amused, but uncomfortable that I had said something stupid without knowing what it was.

Finally, she regained enough control to apologize. "I'm sorry, but you were just so earnest I couldn't deal with it. As I said, to get to the front, you had to be clever. Well, one of the young journalists, Abigail Nichols, had the idea to dress like a man. Abigail was especially pretty. Men who saw her were often transfixed, like the Sirens of Homer. But so were women. I know because I'm as straight as they come. Abigail—well, she did things that no man could do. She was the perfect lesbian. She took the name Seymour Van Dyke as a way of flaunting her sexual orientation to the males in charge of issuing passes. No one ever caught on. And now a half a century later, the joke is still fresh and funny."

"See more from dyke," I said shaking my head. "So who was Abigail Nichols?"

"She didn't talk much about her family. When she got back from a concentration camp, she said something like, 'I'm sure my father would be proud of what the Nazis did at that camp.' I can still hear her saying it because it was an odd thing to say, and the way she said it seemed so casual. We weren't immune to the horrors we saw and never joked about them, so it struck me when she said it. When I asked her what she meant, she just laughed and insisted we go for a drink."

"What happened to her after the war?"

Luci shrugged. "I stayed in touch for a few years, but then she stopped writing. It was 1952. I remember because that's when I graduated from medical school. I sent her an invitation for my graduation, but she never responded."

"Have you ever met a woman named Jennifer Rice?"

"I read some of her travel books, but we never met."

Luci stood up. "You need to go, and I need a nap. Call me if you have any other questions."

She walked me to the door. Certain I'd learned something meaningful but unable to grasp what it was, I stepped outside into a cloud of snow. What I couldn't foresee was that I was now on a path into a past hidden for more than fifty years—a past that some people were determined would never be revealed.

CHAPTER 5
Tuesday, February 12
Wednesday, February 13

Getting out of the city was tedious. As is often the case, all the folks who chose to ignore the forecast decided to head home at the same time. The ones who had stayed home from work decided to go shopping while the others were bailing from work. The result was gridlock. The streets were snarled and the salt trucks, which had been waiting for hours, were rendered useless.

The interstates were easier to negotiate. Trucks loaded with salt and pushing plows spread across all of the lanes of I-66 to dispatch the fallen snow. When the snow immediately began to cover the pavement, another fleet of trucks took over. The storm, it seemed, had met its match. But as I traveled west, the snow fell faster than it could be plowed. An SUV changed lanes too quickly, spun out, hit the median, then another car. Traffic stopped and the snow piled up. I assisted other drivers with the injured until police and paramedics arrived, but the opportunity to beat the storm home passed.

That I reached the poor farm at all was something of a miracle. A chance encounter with a pickup truck sporting a snow plow and a driver willing to take two hundred dollars to carve a path to my front door was all that saved me. Even so, it was after midnight. The power was off, the house was cold, and the kitties were pissed. I fed them and built a fire. The five of us slept in a heap on the floor while the storm raged outside.

The snow fell through the night. I awoke at sunrise and ventured out on the porch. The snow was lighter now, the small flakes swirling on their way to the ground. All totaled, another fifteen inches had been added to the snow pack. A gusty north wind whipped the new snow into impressive drifts, then sculpted them with a delicate touch. If there hadn't been so much of it, I might have thought it beautiful.

The electricity was still off. I had no heat, no telephone service, and no internet connection. More importantly, I needed to drain the water from the pipes to keep them from freezing. I also needed to look in on my neighbor, Gloria, to be certain she was managing. I was eager to process what I had learned about Seymour Van Dyke, but that endeavor would have to wait a bit longer.

I used a camping stove to make coffee and eggs, then donned a winter coat, gloves, and boots, and headed outside. The wind was sharp and penetrating, swirling the snow into blinding white clouds. I shoveled the snow off the porch and made a path to the well house. I shut off the pump and opened the drain valve, then headed to the north pasture. Here, the wind had redistributed the snow, exposing brown grass where the land was flat while creating thick drifts where the land sloped upward. The patchy snow cover gave the field an uncertain look, much like a snake in mid-molt.

Gloria Strap lived on the other side of Lynn Run, a small stream that marked the eastern border of my farm. Her house was set behind a berm that provided some protection when Lynn Run left its banks in the spring.

Visiting Gloria was difficult under any circumstance. She was in her late seventies and passing through the early stages of dementia. Her head was filled with ghosts of family and friends who had hurt her, misunderstood her, and abandoned her for no reason she could articulate. When the ghosts visited her, she devolved into inconsolable sobbing. When lucid, she could tell fascinating stories about Lyle and its residents in decades past. Winter seemed to make her short-term memory worse. I'd asked Doc if cabin fever had something to do with it, but he told me her mind was slowly failing her and that, at some point, she would have to be institutionalized.

I spend enough time dealing with my own demons that I wasn't anxious to deal with Gloria's. But despite my reluctance, I trudged forward. I saw her through the bay window at the back of her house. She was sitting in a chair, wrapped in a blanket, her hands folded in her lap. Gloria, like Luci Turnbull, wore her age with elegance and grace. She had a thick mantel of snow-white hair, beautiful skin, and a gentle figure. Soft lines gave her face character, but she had been spared the wrinkles and loose skin of her contemporaries. What time had spared her body it had taken from her brain. Gloria would lose her identity long before she lost her life or her beauty.

I studied her for a moment, her eyes frozen in a vacant stare. I tapped on the glass, but she remained motionless. I hurried to the front door and stepped inside, unsure what I would find. Cold air greeted me, but the smell of death did not. When I knelt in front of Gloria's chair, she gazed at me. "I don't remember you," she said.

"You will," I said. "You're freezing," I added, squeezing her hands.

Gloria said nothing while I started a fire in her woodstove. The draft was good and the wood dry. In a few minutes, the black metal clicked and clanked to life. I put a pot of water on the stove and, while it heated, rubbed her hands. When it whistled, I made her a cup of tea and sat next to her.

"Has Roslyn been here?" asked Gloria.

"I'm sorry. I'm not sure who you're talking about."

"Of course you do, unless you're getting as forgetful as me. She's my sister. She played with you when you visited the old poor farm."

I remembered a woman of little patience with children who was quick to criticize and scold.

"Of course, Roslyn," I replied.

Gloria finished her tea. I took her cup, and she smiled at me. "I'm sorry, Shep. You'd think I'd remember you of all people." She sighed. "I know what's happening to me. I've seen what it does. That's not how I plan on dying."

"You haven't lost yet," I said.

I checked Gloria's generator and saw that it had been left in manual mode. "That damn thing costs too much money to run," she said, "and it's too damn loud." I convinced her to let me turn it on and to leave it in auto mode. Moments later, the furnace kicked in and the lights came on. I warmed Gloria's breakfast in the microwave and watched her eat it. As I left, I wondered how I'd cope with her reality.

———————————

By the time I headed back, the wind had shifted to the south. The light falling snow was now rain mixed with sleet. As I arrived at my front porch, I heard the throaty growl of a diesel engine approaching. I turned and saw a plume of snow moving toward me. A few minutes later, the noise stopped and the plume dissipated, revealing the pickup truck that had rescued me the night before. The door opened and a burly thirty-year-old with a pony tail and an earring stepped out. He nodded and said, "Markus is the name. I was just down the road a piece so I thought I'd come by and see how you were doing."

I offered him a cup of coffee and invited him inside. Markus was a far cry from a chatty guy, seeming to prefer to communicate with head nods. He followed me into the kitchen, where his attention was drawn to two cats hovering around the refrigerator. "Probably a mouse," I said.

A long groan suggested that Markus thought otherwise. He grasped the fridge and twisted it away from the wall. Another sigh, and then he actually spoke, "That's a problem," he said pointing. I followed his hand to a dimple in the floor, then followed his gaze to a bulge in the ceiling. "Outside," he said, taking a mug and walking away.

With coffee in hand, we stepped onto the porch into a heavy fog that clung to the snowpack, obscuring everything beyond twenty feet away. The air temperature, which just a few hours ago had been in the twenties, was now almost fifty.

"Don't be fooled," said Markus. "The cold and snow are coming back tonight. If it's heavy, I'll be back in the morning to keep your driveway open."

We worked through the crusted snow to where we could see the line where the roof joined the back wall of the house. The line was reasonably straight before a noticeable dip could be seen a few feet on either side of the kitchen. "Most of the year, I'm a contractor," said Markus. "I've got a pretty good idea of what's happening, but I'd like to check the basement."

The basement seemed less foreboding this time, with Markus leading the way. I stood by the steps and watched the beam of his flashlight move and pause, then move again. Each time the light stopped, I heard a soft "yup" confirming some undisclosed conclusion.

A few minutes later, Markus joined me at the foot of the stairs. The power had come on and the oil furnace rumbled into operation. "Lucky for you your cats were playing with a ball. The crack in the foundation is new and it's only going to get bigger. Looks like you're moving,"

"Can't you jack it up or something?" I asked.

"I could. I wouldn't. We would need to pour footers along that back wall. I'd need jack hammers to get through this clay, and the vibration alone might bring it down. This old house isn't worth killing someone. It's trying to die. You should let it."

"How soon?" The question sounded eerily like a question asked of a doctor issuing bad news.

"Tonight. Next year. Maybe never." Markus looked at me. "You won't get any warning. My opinion is that if you stay in this house, eventually you'll be buried under it. I'll install a temporary support along the middle beam. Once that's in, you can move your stuff out. Keep in mind that the support will cause the weight to shift to other beams. The support will eventually fail, and the house will implode. With the rain adding to the weight of the snow on the roof, it may happen sooner rather than later."

In its time as an operating poor farm, the main house had been the residence of a caretaker and his wife. The residents slept in a bunkhouse just behind and to the left of the main dwelling. The current bunkhouse was in very good condition. Individual bedrooms were connected to a large living space fitted with a glass-enclosed fireplace. A common kitchen and dining room adjoined the main room. The bunkhouse had been renovated to accommodate Kikora, a young chimpanzee I was compelled to care for last fall, meaning that some of the doors had been nailed closed and bars fitted in the windows. To keep Kikora out, the furniture had been pushed into the kitchen and a divider fashioned. The bunkhouse was not in shape for me to move in, and I wasn't skilled enough to remodel it by myself.

I called Heartwood House and explained the situation to Cecil. Cecil didn't say much other than, "okay," leaving me wondering if he understood the problem I was describing. An hour later, Sheriff Belamy's black SUV crept up the rutted road to the house. Harry and Cecil nodded, took their tools, and went to work in the bunkhouse. Robbie and Frieda carried baskets of food inside.

Sheriff Belamy stared at me and laughed. "Shit happens to you more than anyone I know."

The sheriff and I busied ourselves clearing snow from the bunkhouse. Markus' red pickup arrived a half hour later. He retreated to the back of his truck and walked into the house with a long metal post and a few tools. Twenty minutes later, he came out.

"That there's a death trap," he said, "but you should be good for a little bit. I need to show you what I've done and what you need to do while you're moving out."

I followed Markus into the basement. He must have had the eyes of a cat because I almost lost him in the shadows near the old boiler. When I found him, he was standing next to a metal post that extended from the floor to the ceiling.

"This here jack is holding up your house, at least for now. But because it's sitting on dirt, you're going to need to adjust it every now and again." He pointed to a large box wrench fitted over a nut. "You turn this clockwise until it gets real tight. Too tight and you may overload the beam at the other end." He moved his finger to a metal bar. "This is what you push if you was going to release the jack. You don't want to do that. You don't want to touch that 'cause the beam here will move and, once it starts, it won't stop. You see what I'm saying?"

"Turn that one, but not that one," I said.

"That's about it," agreed Markus. "If you hear a cracking noise, get your butt up the stairs real quick like. Of course, she may not give you a warning and just drop on your head." A moment passed, and Markus slapped me on the back. "I'm just fooling with you."

"You had me going there," I said, amazed at how social Markus had become. "One more thing. You have mice, maybe rats, getting in here. Don't take much of a crack for them beggars to sneak inside. You don't want them to get into your stuff before you move it." He clicked on a flashlight and scanned the joists just behind the boiler. "I put a couple of traps up there where I saw droppings on top of your duct work. If they get snapped, you'll smell 'em."

I followed Markus to his truck. He offered to take down the house once it was empty and I accepted.

The hardest task was to clear the snow and ice from the well house to turn on the water to the bunkhouse. Belamy helped me free the lid and watched as I climbed down a short ladder. At least in the winter, I didn't have to worry about copperheads. The water ran muddy for a while. I waited until it cleared, then turned on the water heater.

As the temperature dropped again, Belamy and I dug a path from the main house to the bunkhouse. I moved small appliances, clothes, boxes of books, personal papers, electronic equipment, and anything I could grab to the porch. I couldn't believe that I could have accumulated so much stuff in a year. Harry, Belamy, and I hauled it all to my new home. At my direction, the poor farm's historical documents were stacked along the wall in the main room. I put the papers relating to Jennifer Rice's murder on the small café table near the fireplace. Frieda had found pictures of my mother and Reilly Heartwood and placed them on the mantel.

As the first flakes of new snow started to fall, Belamy insisted that the work was done for the day. I had water, heat, electricity, a functional kitchen, a bedroom, and a bath. The rest could wait.

Robbie helped Frieda, Cecil, and Harry load Belamy's SUV for the trip back to town. I turned toward the old farmhouse, which was a dark, lonely shape in the fog of falling snow. Sadness gripped me, but I drew in a breath and willed the feeling away. The Residents and this farm are all that connect me to my past. Growing up, I didn't know Reilly was my father, but I guess at some level I did. This is one of the places where he played with me. He taught me to see the poor people here as family. I remember the smell of bacon and apple pie coming from the kitchen. I remember being told ghost stories by some of the older men and jumping into the hay from the top of the barn. The people I knew then, except for the Residents, are all dead. The old house became my sanctuary, the first place I'd felt safe after leaving prison, and it was dying, too.

When I turned away from the old house, the SUV departed. Robbie, standing a few feet from me, was watching me. "Are you okay?"

"I was just thinking how pretty the old house looks," I said.

Robbie gave me a doubtful look. "I'm cold and need something to drink. We're going to go inside and you're going to explain to me why you failed to let me know about your trip to visit Gus. After you are appropriately contrite, you will tell me what you learned yesterday."

I followed Robbie into the bunkhouse. She sat on a carpet in front of the fireplace. While I lit a fire, I described my visits with Gus, Zak, and Luci. She made faces but said nothing. I joined her and we watched silently until the logs were engulfed in flames.

"So," she said, "if I get this right, we have three sets of photographs, all taken by women: Abigail Nichols, also known as Seymour Van Dyke; an unnamed woman who came to the farm with a baby; and Jennifer Rice, the one who was murdered. They aren't connected by any physical evidence other than the pictures, but you are focused on them because you believe you might be able tease a motive for murder by discovering how they are related. Does that about sum it all up?"

"Pretty much."

Robbie sat quietly, the glow from the embers painting her face in flickering hues of orange and red. She twirled her index finger around her thumb, signaling she was considering the new information, a process I had learned not to interrupt. The process ended when she said, "Doc and the sheriff asked me to stay behind to make sure you don't get involved in Jennifer Rice's murder. They don't mind if you want to know who took the pictures at the farm. And it's okay if you want to identify the lady with the baby, how she came to have it, why she was so eager to get away when Doc called the cops, and what happened to the child afterwards. Actually, I suspect they want you to do those things. What they don't want is for you to be wondering who killed Jennifer Rice. They want you to accept that Albert Loftus did it."

"So you're like a double agent," I said.

"Almost fifty years ago, a woman brought a light brown baby here. She may have sat close to where we are sitting now, thinking about her future. I can't imagine how tormented she was. I can't tell you why it bothers me so much that she seems to have disappeared without a trace."

Another sigh and she stared into the fire. "I think about Jennifer Rice being beaten to death. No one should get away with beating up an elderly woman. No one. I want be certain that Albert killed her. Reggie said he and the detective in charge of the case weren't certain, that there were holes in the case. The cops don't know what we know, and we can't tell them because Reggie's our client. So if Albert didn't kill her, it's up to us to find out who did. I can't explain why, but that's where I'm parked."

When I didn't respond, she glowered at me. "Don't even think about reciting that male gibberish about not wanting me to get hurt, blah, blah, blah," she said in a dismissive tone. "I can probably shoot better than you and run faster."

"You were always one to stand your ground," I said.

"I'm serious, Shep. I want to do this."

With a poker, I pushed a log, sending a shower of embers flying up the chimney. "The way this works," I said, "is that we identify people who might know something about the victim. If they're cooperative, they name others and so on. The danger comes from asking the wrong person the right question. But the hardest part is what to do with the answers. We have to decide what we do with what we know. We have to make choices, and sometimes its feels like playing God. Doing the right thing isn't as easy as it sounds."

"I can handle it," she said confidently.

I poked at the log again to give the impression I was doing something useful. Robbie sounded confident about an undertaking she had never taken on. I had survived two quests for the truth involving murders. I wasn't so sure I was up to doing it again.

I closed the glass doors to the fireplace and took her hand. "Well, then, there you have it."

CHAPTER 6
Thursday, February 14

The events of the day had left me exhausted. With snow falling, I had little interest in driving Robbie home. Robbie agreed to stay, but only if I agreed to behave myself. I offered her my room, but she wasn't happy about me sleeping on the floor.

"We're adults," she said. "Just keep your hands to yourself and your clothes on and we can share the same bed."

On other occasions, we had made the same deal, only to find that our hands wandered and things happened. But tonight all I wanted was a good night's sleep.

Even that proved elusive, however, but not for any Robbie reasons.

A little after midnight, my cellphone rang. Robbie rolled over to my side of the bed and handed it to me, then watched anxiously as I answered it. Late night calls rarely bring good news, and I am predisposed to think the worst. Thoughts about the Residents of the poor farm, Frieda, Doc, and my aunt topped the list. So I was both relieved and annoyed when I heard Zak's voice asking, "Are you busy?"

I answered with an even, "No," and waited.

Robbie made a face, and I mouthed Zak's name. She turned her head so she could hear what Zak was saying.

"I just called to tell you I was wrong about the photographs taken at your farm and the travel photos shot by Jennifer Rice being taken with the same camera."

"So they weren't taken by the same person," I said, doing my best to hide my disappointment.

"That's not what I said. I said I was wrong, I didn't say how I was wrong."

Communicating with Zak was never easy. Patience was mandatory.

But tonight I wasn't in the mood for one of Zak's games.

"How about you tell me what you meant, and we'll call it a night?"

Predictably, the phone went silent. I had bruised Zak's sensitive ego and needed to make nice.

"Sometimes being wrong is a good thing," I said, "especially when the way you're wrong matters."

"For crying out loud," whispered Robbie.

She was about to return to her side of the bed when Zak started speaking.

"So, I played with the photos all last night. The FBI's got this really sweet computer with multiple processors and photo analytic software. I thought there was a glitch with the software because the results I was getting made no sense. But the results were fine. It was my expectations that were causing the problems. Do you see how that happens?"

"Expectations can ruin a new day," I said.

"What does that mean?" asked Zak.

"I was agreeing with you. So about the results?"

"Well, I was trying to determine if the travel photos and the photos of the poor farm were taken by the same camera. I used the Seymour Van Dyke images as a control, assuming they were taken by a different camera. But here's the kicker. They weren't. All of the photos were taken by the same camera. You can draw whatever conclusions you want, but I'd say they were taken by the same person. Kind of cool, don't you think?"

The revelation took a moment to sink in. What had started as a story about three people was now a story about one. Jennifer Rice, Seymour Van Dyke, AKA Abigail Nichols, and the woman with the baby were all the same person.

"Very," I said.

I thanked Zak and ended the call. I waited for Robbie to pummel me with questions, but she rolled onto her back and stared into space. After a moment, she said, "You couldn't have made this up. A young woman, a lesbian, who once pretended to be a man so she could take war photographs, kidnaps a brown baby, changes her name, and fades into history, until she is savagely beaten to death fifty years later. I imagine she had lots of secrets."

I turned on a light and headed to the living room to retrieve my laptop. The felines followed me back into the bedroom, and one by one made their way onto the bed.

I handed the computer to Robbie. "We have a small problem," I said. "How small?"

"I believe we have no heat, and the fire has gone out," I said. "I'm guessing it's about fifty-five degrees in the living room and going down"

"If your feet are cold, stay on your side of the bed and don't touch me. Okay? According to the internet there's an Abigail Nichols, a teacher, who was charged with having sex with one of her students, and another is an actress who performs in summer theater in New Hope, Connecticut when she's not busy as postmaster."

"Keep in mind that our Abigail was seventy-seven and is, sadly, muerto."

"With that in mind, I searched 'Nichols' and 'Virginia' and got a hit on a Dr. Alton Nichols who was the director of The Sweetwater Hospital and Institute for Epileptics and the Feebleminded. Sweetwater is located near Charlottesville."

"That's where Baby John was born."

"Dr. Nichols was also an internationally renowned eugenicist," continued Robbie, "whatever that is."

The first time I'd heard of eugenics was in a constitutional law class. I hadn't heard the term since and had no clue who Dr. Nichols was.

"The hospital can't be a coincidence," I said.

"He and his wife Connie had two children—Willet and Abigail," answered Robbie. "So, I think we've found the right family. Nothing on Abigail, but a lot has been written about Alton Nichols. You can hear a short biography, some unflattering but unproven accusations about how he treated patients, or how family members want his name restored to historical markers as a famous Virginian."

"I'll take biography," I said, "as long as it's short."

"Alton Nichols was born in 1892. He went to medical school and graduated with honors, which wasn't hard considering that in many of our medical schools you weren't required to have a high school diploma. In 1916, he helped establish the Sweetwater Hospital and Institute for Epileptics and the Feebleminded. The hospital took its name from the town of Sweetwater, which at one time had been a thriving community of tobacco and corn farmers. The jewel of the town had been the Oakfield Plantation. Without slave labor, the crops were too expensive to grow. The whites with money hung on. Ex-slaves who were too old to enjoy emancipation stayed behind to care for their ex-masters and grow old with them. Pig farming and logging allowed a small group of blacks to eke out a living, but Sweetwater ceased to matter. Just before World War I, Oakfield Plantation was sold for the construction of a hospital 'dedicated to the improvement of humanity through science.' The building of the hospital revitalized the town."

"Interesting in a who-cares kind of way and not exactly short," I said.

"Don't get all cranky," snapped Robbie. "I'm just getting to the good parts. Nichols became increasingly interested in eugenics, a social movement masquerading as science that advocated the improvement of the human race through selective breeding and sterilization. In the early twenties, he became the face of a campaign to remove defective genes from the gene pool. He believed that with proper breeding, the curse of mental illness, homosexuality, criminal behavior, promiscuity, alcoholism, and even poverty could be eliminated in two generations. Basically, he wanted humans to be bred like livestock." Robbie glanced at me, then scowled at the computer screen. "This guy was a racist jerk"

"Is there anything else?"

"Dr. Nichols was a firm believer in the supremacy of the white race, and eugenics provided a scientific basis for his racist beliefs. Blah, blah, blah. He ran for the Virginia legislature and led the effort to enact the racial integrity act and the sterilization act. The former prohibited interracial marriage, and the other allowed the state to sterilize those considered unfit to reproduce."

"I'm sure you studied Buck v. Bell in law school," I said. "Carrie Buck was a poor white woman who, following a rape, gave birth to a baby girl. The Commonwealth of Virginia had decided to sterilize her under its Racial Integrity Act of 1924. In 1927, the U.S. Supreme Court issued an opinion upholding the constitutionality of the law. Justice Oliver Wendell Holmes remarked that 'three generations of imbeciles is enough.' Carrie went on to help others until she died in 1983. The daughter she had before she was sterilized was of average intelligence and died at age eight. Neither her mother nor her daughter was an imbecile, but of course, no one ever apologized for the suffering they caused them."

"What good would an apology have done her?" asked Robbie angrily. She refocused on the computer screen. "More blah, blah, blah. Let's see. During the thirties, he corresponded with Nazi scientists who, as he put it, 'were not constrained by short-sighted concepts that elevated the rights of the individual above the rights of the majority,' and could use human subjects to affirm 'what we already know is true.' He continued to head Sweetwater until his death in 1955. A few years ago, the governor of Virginia issued an apology to those forcefully sterilized and ordered Nichols' name to be removed from government institutions and historical markers."

I looked over to see two felines staking out spots next to Robbie's feet. One was curled up next to her head. The fourth had found her hand and was getting an ear rubbed. "I'm assuming you were paraphrasing?"

"The racism part was admittedly editorializing, but I submit that he earned it."

"And what are the unproven allegations?"

Robbie's fingers danced over the keys of the laptop. "Okay. It seems that he may have performed tests on some of his mental patients. He denied injecting the blood of a schizophrenic patient into a normal patient. He also denied sterilizing black women and men admitted to Sweetwater for other procedures." Robbie closed the laptop and tossed it on the bed. "Of course. Let's erect statues and plaster the state with historical markers celebrating this asshole's life and accomplishments. He hates blacks and women, and he was friends with Nazi war criminals. I think he should be nominated for fucking sainthood."

"Your restraint is admirable."

I was staring at the ceiling, when Robbie poked me with her finger. "Tell me what you're thinking."

"Reggie told us a story about Baby John being stolen from Sweetwater Hospital. Now we know that the guy who ran the hospital was not just a racist but a man bent on purifying the white race. What I'm trying to get my head around is the likelihood that Baby John was not the only child to be reported dead. We've stepped into something bigger than Reggie and his cousins, and I'm not sure what to make of it."

Robbie handed me my phone. "You need to call Reggie. He needs to hear this. And turn on the speaker so I can hear it."

Reggie answered on the first ring. "Tell me you found something?" "It's Nick and Nora Charles," I said. For some reason, that line popped into my head because the warden at the prison loved the Thin Man series. From the look on Robbie's face and the silence at the other end of the phone, the allusion was lost on others. "The woman who took the pictures was Abigail Nichols."

"Okay, but who is she?"

"She is Seymour Van Dyke and Jennifer Rice"

"You lost me," said Reggie.

"Abigail Nichols used those names as aliases. There is only one photographer. Presumably, she was the one who took Baby John. She left the poor farm with the baby and assumed the name Jennifer Rice."

Reggie was silent for a moment. "So the person who stole Baby John is dead?"

"I'm afraid so."

"So that's the end of that?"

"Not quite," said Robbie. "Abigail's father was the superintendent of the hospital where your cousin was born. We think Abigail took your cousin to the farm. We don't know why, but it may have been to protect him. Your aunt's experience may not be an isolated one. We'd like to find out."

I put my hand over the phone. "Since when did we decide to find out?" I said.

"We decided a second before I said we did," whispered Robbie.

"You know where this is leading, Shep. You start asking questions about Abigail Nichols," said Reggie, "and whoever killed her may decide that you're a threat. I can't let you do that. I'll speak with Detective Hunter and we'll do this by the book."

"And what? Confess to all your felonies and misdemeanors?" I asked.

"That's not a smart move. We can follow up on what we've learned and see if we can find your cousin. It won't take long to check out the few leads we have. Albert Loftus isn't going to be any worse off if you wait a few more days."

"He's right," said Robbie. "I know it's hard to grasp, but he is."

"If you want to find your cousin, you're going to have to let us do this," I added.

Reggie was quiet for a long time. "Just see what you can find out about Baby John. Don't be asking questions about Abigail. Promise me. Okay?"

"You know I can't do that and also find Baby John."

"Shit. I have a bad feeling about this, but okay. Just try not to do anything stupid."

I couldn't promise that either, but agreed anyway and hung up.

With the call ended, the only sound in the room was soft purring. A glance from Robbie confirmed that she too was aware that Reggie's favor had become more complicated and risky. "When I agreed to help Reggie, I didn't see this coming," she said finally.

"I need to light a fire," I said.

Robbie, having wrapped herself in a blanket, followed me into the living room and was hovering while I stirred the fireplace coals. "You're thinking about something," she said. "It's impolite not to share."

"We have no reason to think that Albert Loftus didn't kill Abigail Nichols other than Reggie saying it didn't feel right. But let's assume for a moment that Albert is innocent. We don't know who murdered Abigail Nichols and, more importantly, we don't know why. It's possible that the kidnapping of Reggie's cousin plays into her killing. So, just asking about Baby John may not keep us from getting into trouble with the person who beat her to death."

"So, are you saying that we shouldn't ask any questions about Baby John?"

I tossed a log into the fireplace and it bounced out. "I think we have to be honest about what we're really trying to accomplish. Reggie asked us to find the photographer who took pictures at the poor farm. We've done that. He also said that unless he knew for certain that Albert was the killer, he would go to the police. We can't pretend that we aren't trying to figure out who murdered Jennifer Rice, AKA Abigail Nichols. If we want to keep Reggie out of jail, that's what we need to do. I know what I just told him, but I'm not sure you fully appreciate what I've volunteered you to do. I'm not being macho, but Reggie is right about the risks involved in asking questions about Abigail and Baby John. If we aren't up to the task, then we need to call Reggie back and tell him."

I heard Robbie take a long deep breath. "You know better than anyone that Reggie can't go to prison. A black cop would look like fresh meat to the other inmates. I can't tell you I'm not scared, but I think this is something we need to do."

"And the estate taxes?"

"We have a few weeks. You can work nights if you have to"

"Then it's decided," I said.

"So where do we start?"

The log caught quickly. With the fire started, I grabbed a folder from the café table and removed the photograph of Doc sitting on a bale of hay with the young woman I now knew was Abigail Nichols. With her identity revealed, she seemed sadder to me, almost desperate. Doc was pointing at her, threatening to expose her. I handed the picture to Robbie.

"Why did she take the baby?" I asked.

"From what little we know, Abigail was a worldly, confident woman. She traveled, loved adventure, and wasn't likely to settle down. I can't see her as a lonely lesbian stealing a child to satisfy some biological imperative. If Abigail wanted a child, she'd have one. But no, she committed a felony by kidnapping a baby. I want to know why she took the child, where she went after leaving the poor farm, what happened to that baby, and what happened to the baby's parents. How did a white woman manage to travel with a child that wasn't white? Who took care of that baby? Where is he now? And I want to know if anyone other than Albert Loftus had a reason to beat her to death."

"Okay," said Robbie slowly. "How do we do that?"

"Ask questions, get names of people who might have known her, and get lucky."

"And where would you go to ask your questions?"

"Sweetwater. I'd go to Sweetwater."

Robbie took my hand. "Then let's go check out Sweetwater Hospital and the house where Abigail lived. It probably won't lead to anything, but we need to start somewhere."

"You sure?"

"We have a friend in trouble and I have questions begging for answers. I'm sure."

"I suppose we could drive over to Sweetwater tomorrow if the storm isn't too bad. If we travel during the daylight, we should be okay."

Robbie gave me a soft peck on the cheek. "A Valentine's Day date at a mental institution. Not every girl receives an offer like that."

I laughed. "Be careful. I might leave you there."

CHAPTER 7
Thursday, February 14

I brought mattresses and pillows into the main room and laid them in front of the fireplace. Robbie, the felines, and I awoke before sunrise in a pile of intertwined bodies and balls of purring fur. Only hunger and the need to relieve ourselves pulled us from our warm covers.

The problem with the heat was simple but not easy to solve. The oil tank for the bunkhouse was not connected to the tank for the main house. The main house, which had been abandoned, had plenty of oil, while the bunkhouse we occupied had none. Getting the oil from one tank to the other required a pump, which I didn't have. The snow that had fallen over night was relatively light but enough to keep an oil truck from attempting my driveway. I called my new friend Markus, and he promised he would find a pump suitable for the task. In the meantime, we huddled around the fireplace and wore layers to ward off the chill.

I set a plate of pancakes and sausage on the café table. Robbie said little as she smothered a stack of cakes and a sausage patty in maple syrup. "This is good," she said with her mouth full.

"I worked in the kitchen in prison. You'd be surprised by what can be done with weevil-infested flour and mysterymeat."

"While you were cooking, I looked up Sweetwater. The hospital and the Nichols home were sold to the Anderson Historical Foundation. From what I can tell, nothing has been done to renovate the hospital or tear it down, but it's surrounded by a fence. I bet we could sneak in and have a look around. And the Nichols family residence is nearby, apparently uninhabited. That might be fun to explore."

"Nothing like a day of breaking and entering and trespassing to reset one's moral compass."

Sweetwater was a little more than a hundred miles from Lyle. To the lengths of old carpet I kept in my car, we added a snow shovel and headed out. Robbie insisted on going by her house for a quick shower and a change of clothes.

When she returned to my car, she opened a book and ignored me. I worked my way through a labyrinth of narrow, snow-covered roads until I reached Route 29 South. Just as we entered Charlottesville, Robbie slammed the book closed and tossed it onto the backseat. "I hate a book with a stupid ending," she announced.

"You mean where things don't work out?"

"No, where everything works out just right. Life isn't like that. It never adds up completely."

"Maybe," I said, "the writer was just trying to give the reader a break from the real world."

"If I'd wanted to read a romance, I would have bought one. Anyway, I didn't mean to be rude, but I had to finish the last few chapters. Of course, now I wish I hadn't bothered."

"That makes two of us," I said agreeably.

I took the exit for Route 250 West, then turned on Brook Road. Thirty minutes later, the GPS announced that we'd reached our destination. Our arrival was confirmed by a sign riddled with bullet holes welcoming us to Sweetwater, advising that the speed limit was twenty-five, and warning that the limit was "enforced by radar." The sign begged the question, "By whom?"

We cruised slowly down Main Street, which curiously had been plowed. Fresh snow was piled up against windows and doors of empty buildings, the feeling of desolation enhanced by clouds of white teased from roofs and snow drifts by a swirling wind. A Western Auto store still had a banner in its window offering "Radio Flyer Wagons." What I guessed had been a drugstore displayed a "Drink a bite to eat at 10-2 and 4" ad for Dr. Pepper. But most of the buildings were marked by broken windows, and a few looked to have been charred by fire. If we'd come to ask questions about Abigail Nichols, it appeared that we'd wasted our time. Sweetwater was a ghost town.

I considered turning around when a stocky man wearing a pair of ski pants and a leather jacket stepped into the street and waved us to a stop. He sauntered to the window of my car, the top of a ski hat white from a passing snow shower. I rolled down the window and he peered in. A patch on the shoulder of his jacket announced that he worked for Blue Ridge Security.

"'Ma'am," he said, nodding in Robbie's direction.

"Was I speeding?" I asked deferentially.

"Most of the time I'd take that question as an admission of guilt. But, truthfully I don't care whether you were or not. I do want to know what you're doing here. You don't look like a rock thrower or a druggie, so more than likely you're just lost."

"Actually," said Robbie leaning across me, "we're looking into a murder."

I was dismayed at Robbie's bluntness and certain that the man at my window would reconsider his conclusion about drug use.

"You're messing with me," he said, a broad grin on his face.

When we didn't speak, he clapped his hands together. "Hot damn! You're serious! Man, I gotta hear this one. My name's Kyle Hopper by the way. How about you tell me the details over a cup of coffee and cinnamon roll?"

We introduced ourselves, then pulled next to his SUV. We followed him toward a brick building, the word "Sheriff" still faintly visible on the glass window of the door. I took Robbie's arm and said, "I thought the plan was to not draw attention to ourselves."

"The plan was to ask questions. If anyone knows who's around here, it's Kyle, though I will admit I have doubts about following him inside."

Kyle turned and apparently sensed her hesitation. "I'm sorry. I've apparently frightened you. You meet a strange man in a ghost town who wants to lead you to a strange and dark place. It's very Stephen King, I think. If you would like to take a picture of my driver's license and send it to someone at home, that would be fine. But I'm sure you appreciate that there is a genre of horror movies in which two handsome young people come to a town to terrorize an old man before they eat him. So, I would ask to do the same. Kind of a draw, you see."

"I'm sorry," said Robbie.

"Don't be," said Kyle, opening the door. "Fear operates to keep you alive. With more data, you'll relax and so will I. Until then, I won't personalize your wariness if you don't mine."

We stepped inside and were greeted by a blast of warm, humid air courtesy of a large iron pot of steaming water that rested on a wood burning stove. "I get sinus infections from the dry air. I should go to Florida, but then there would be no one left to watch my town."

"Your town?" asked Robbie, handing me her coat.

"Well, not mine, although it feels like that sometimes. The Anderson Historical Foundation owns this building, the hospital, and a few of the homes. I think they had some crazy idea to restore the mansion where the hospital is located and open a spa. Lots of hot springs nearby and it's really pretty in the fall. Maybe it sounded like a good idea after a lot of drinking, but I'm not the one with the money, you see? About five years ago, they hired me to watch the place and to keep the dopers out of things. I don't have a family, so being here alone wasn't too bad and the money was good. But five years is about the limit, you know? I'll probably change my mind when spring arrives. I complain every winter and always re-enlist after spring comes. Go figure."

"Any chance we could see the Sweetwater Hospital?" I asked.

"I'm not supposed to give tours. Insurance lawyers get nervous about people walking around the old hospital, but maybe we can take a look. I really want to hear about your murder." Kyle pointed to a door. "My living quarters are actually in the cell block. I'm telling you that just so you won't be startled by the jail cells. I think you'll find it pretty cool when you see it."

I tossed our coats on a bench by the front door. We followed Kyle through a heavy door down a hallway formed from cinder block walls and a concrete floor and ceiling. About ten feet from the door, the hallway turned left. Just in front of us was a jail cell, its heavy bars speckled with peeling green paint. A cot, a sink, and a toilet were visible in the dusky light. I spent a few months in a cell much like this one before being transferred to a federal minimum security prison. The memory was not welcomed. As we made the left turn, I noticed a small sign that read, "GUEST ROOM" hanging from the lock.

Here, the hallway was carpeted, and the walls covered in tiles of soft earth tones. The bars had been removed from a row of four cells and two of them connected together.

"This," said Kyle, pointing to the first cell, "is where I keep my coffee and espresso machine and a wet bar. Next is the kitchen and breakfast nook. I love to cook and, obviously, eat. Finally, this is the security room, which was created from two cells. I have three of those new flat-panel monitors, a satellite connection, and recliners arranged stadium-seating style. Those panels cost more than my house back in Jersey, so the Foundation must have money to waste. With the satellite hook-up and recliners, this room doubles as a theater room. Friends from Charlottesville come over to watch football and college basketball most nights so I don't get too lonely. When the game is good, this place rocks." On each of the monitors was an array of pictures, some of which I recognized as views of Main Street. "The cameras are connected to a video computer that allows me to monitor most of the town, the old hospital, the church, and the few residential properties that haven't been significantly vandalized. The system alerts me when there's motion or heat, so I knew you were coming a few minutes before you arrived."

"The image of that house is flashing red," said Robbie, pointing at the monitor.

"That's the old Nichols residence," he said, selecting an image from inside the house. "Dr. Nichols ran the hospital. Every couple of weeks, his son, Willet, breaks in and rummages through what's left of his parents' personal things. I don't know what he's looking for, and after all these years, he probably doesn't either. I let him have his time, then roust him and send him on his way. He's a druggie and has mental problems. The system is prone to false alarms, so I doubt he's there now." Kyle pressed a button on a remote and the flashing light disappeared.

"That's the tour of my digs, except for my bedroom. That's up front, but it's too messy for showing. So now you owe me a story about a murder and what it has to do with Sweetwater, and I owe you the best cup of coffee and the most scrumptious cinnamon pastry you've ever had."

I took one more look at the monitor before giving in to Kyle's social agenda. The coffee and the roll were as advertised. He listened attentively while I related an abbreviated version of the murder of Jennifer Rice. I indicated that we were tracking down a possible connection between the victim and Sweetwater, but weren't at liberty to provide a lot of details. Kyle asked a few questions, but mostly just listened with his arms folded across his chest. When we were done, he studied each of us for a moment.

"People that come through here see an overweight middle-aged white guy and think I'm a local goober." He smiled and looked at Robbie. "Unless they think I'm a serial killer. The truth is that I once was a detective in New Jersey. I worked too much and got in some trouble with the guys at the station. In the end, I lost my wife to a guy I hired to manage our finances. I took to gambling but never won. The horses, the drinking, and never being home was too much stupidity for any wife to deal with. Now I sit in this town alone eleven months of the year while my kids are being raised by an investment banker." Kyle shook his head. "Now, there I go complaining again."

I motioned to the room with the television monitors. "That's a lot of security for keeping kids out of abandoned buildings."

"You're not kidding," said Kyle. "I send videos to a PO box every week, whether there's anything on them or not. I had a camera on your car five minutes before you hit the edge of town. A picture of your license plate was sent to some place in New Jersey before you reached the end of Main Street. The people that pay me have made it clear that I'm paid to mind my business and do what I'm told, so I don't ask questions. Doesn't mean I don't have them."

"So will you report our visit?" asked Robbie.

"You'll show up on a bunch of cameras, so your being here won't be a secret. What we talk about is none of anyone's business as far as I'm concerned. I'm still not sure why you're here."

I forced a laugh. "You know how these things work. You get a lead that's probably unrelated to what your client wants you to do, but if you don't follow up on it, he sues you for malpractice. We need to see if our murder victim had any connection to this town or the Nichols family so we can move on to something else."

Kyle smiled at us. "And you get to run up those billable hours. Am I right? You're getting paid to eat my rolls and drink my coffee. Fuck me! I should have gone to law school."

"Do you think we could talk to Willet?" asked Robbie.

"He might show up at his family residence again today, but he may not be back until summer. If you go looking for him, you'll never find him. A few folks still live in town who may have known the Nichols family. That's about the best I can do on short notice."

Kyle left the room. I could hear him talking on the phone but couldn't hear what he was saying. I turned to Robbie and whispered, "Are you alright?"

Robbie pursed her lips. "I could have met with a client who wanted to sue his neighbor because the neighbor's dog is crapping in his yard. Instead, I'm in a renovated jail house being served coffee and cake by a man who at worst could be a serial killer or at best is a former resident of the mental institution that we came to visit."

"And you're with me," I said.

"Yes…and there's that."

CHAPTER 8
Thursday, February 14

We had come to Sweetwater to learn about Abigail Nichols and Baby John by breaking into the hospital and the Nichols home. When Robbie volunteered the purpose of our visit to Kyle, I thought the opportunity for stealth was lost. But we had managed to hide from Kyle our interest in Abigail and Baby John behind the mysterious workings of legal practice, and in the process reaped the benefit of an interview with a longtime resident of Sweetwater. All things considered, not a bad outcome.

We climbed into Kyle's SUV. In five minutes, we pulled into the parking lot in front of a small stone church next to a pickup truck. "The church is monitored for video but there's no audio from here, so you can say whatever you want," said Kyle. "If I'm asked, I'll just say you were doing research and that I thought it best to let you look around and be done with it.

"The man in the truck is the Pastor Gaylord Macklin. He's probably seventy, maybe seventy-five, but he looks a lot older. I keep an eye on him and he keeps watch on the church. I'd like to do more for the old church, but I don't have much say in how the foundation's money is spent."

We stepped from the SUV and waited. Gaylord slid out of his truck and slowly stood up, his final position not fully vertical, his weight supported by a carved walking stick.

Kyle introduced us. Gaylord, his eyes clouded by cataracts, stepped close to see my face, then offered me his hand. He had long bronze-colored fingers that were knurled and bent. I squeezed his hand gently to avoid breaking the ancient members, but his grip was strong and almost painful. "My heart is heavy with the news that the Lord has taken an elderly woman from us in a brazen and violent way. I've been told you're doing what you can to see that the Devil takes the son-of-a-bitch who killed her. I'll help you in any way I can."

As we followed Gaylord down a narrow path that cut through the snow-pack around the side of the church, Gaylord's walking stick tapped out the beat of his slow gait. The path ended at the base of an old wall. "This is where the slaves and the descendants of slaves are buried," he said, panning a graveyard with his stick. "The last grave was dug here in 1956."

The new snow lay softly on a web of twisted brambles and vines, and made the neglected graveyard almost pretty. Except for one large marble monument, only a few small headstones were visible through the undergrowth.

"We are surrounded by trees, but this was not always the case." He pointed to his left. "That's where the slaves worked six days a week to grow tobacco. And while you can't see it, what's left of the Oakfield Mansion is just a half a mile up that hill. When the farming stopped, nature was quick to put things back the way God intended. The locust came first, followed by the pines. Maybe God felt bad about the black folk who spent their lives in bondage and got tired of looking at the fields where their blood and sweat was spilt for nothing. Maybe that's why it's all hidden and forgotten."

I pointed at the white monument, but the inscription was hidden by weeds. "Who's buried here?"

Gaylord ignored my question. "I'm cold and I need to go inside."

The inside of the church was lit with candles that danced and flickered in response to some unperceivable draft. The light from the candles cast a warm orange glow that was reflected as a rich golden-brown by the yellow pine walls and benches. The floor was a mosaic of irregular slate stones that ranged from a soft blue to almost black.

"We can't afford to have electricity hooked up all the time, and we don't run the generator unless we have a church service. The roof has started to leak and rats are starting to chew on things, so not too many folk want to bother with the old church these days. Kyle has tried to help, but he's got to handle the problems of that stupid town. Why in God's name anyone would want to own a town is beyond me."

I wanted to ask questions, but I knew better than to seem too eager. Gaylord had an agenda and there was no point in interrupting him.

The pastor slowly made his way up three small steps, pulled himself up onto a tall pulpit, and looked down at the three of us. "Please be seated. The church was built in the 1840s by the slaves who worked at the plantation. The men who worked on it were the most skilled. They had to get permission to use the lumber and stones they found 'cause they belong to the master of Oakfield. When the youngest son took over as head of the household, things got easier. He allowed them use of a wagon and a team of mules to haul what they needed to finish the church."

He pointed a long, crooked finger at me. "Don't go thinking he made life easy," he said angrily, "because he didn't. No sir. He beat them, sold them, and had his way with some of the younger women. But he was a big improvement over his father."

Kyle rubbed the corner of a pew with his hand. "I can't imagine what it would be like, being a slave, being whipped and disrespected every day of your life."

"No, young man, you can't," said the Pastor sternly. "One day a week, for just a few hours, forty slaves filled this structure and prayed that the Lord would take them from bondage and show them a promised land." His voice was strong and passionate and swelled and retreated with a practiced rhythm. "They came when someone died. They came when someone's mamma or daughter was sold. They came when a child was born. On a hot night in August, they might come to lie on the cool stones. And if the master was in a good mood and the harvest made him good money, he would let them come to celebrate. Music would be played and a deer or pig cooked along with sweet potatoes and greens. And then the next day, he'd work them twice as hard to make up for lost time. This was their only refuge—this chapel—when they were breathing. The church cemetery was their refuge when their breathing stopped."

Gaylord's eyes scanned the benches, occasionally nodding his head as if acknowledging each member of a congregation that only he could see. "They're still here, pining for freedom, asking for the same things that men and women of all colors want for themselves and their children. I feel it every time I stand here." He broke his own reverie with a laugh. "Maybe I was here myself in a life before this one."

He moved slowly down from the pulpit. He was carrying a binder and a photograph album, which he handed to Kyle. "I need to sit a spell," he said, parking himself between Robbie and me. "I grew up a member of this church. I've saved photographs and newspaper clippings over the years. I talked to my parents and a lot of the old timers before they died, so I could convince someone that this place needs to be preserved. You hear me? This is not just black slave history. This is American and Virginia history. You see what I'm saying. But no one will listen."

Gaylord worked his jaw while muttering to himself. After a few moments passed, he said, "Kyle said you wanted some information about the Nichols family. The pictures you want to see are toward the back. Dr. Nichols liked to drop by at holidays with his family and hand out hams and turkeys. A white reporter would take a picture of the white doctor with the darkies to prove he wasn't a racist. The members of the church had heard stories about the hospital, about him killing babies and such, and did what they were told."

"Why would he kill babies?" asked Robbie.

"Who knows what makes some white people do what they do? I'm not saying he did. I'm saying that's what we were told."

Kyle stopped at a photograph of a family of white people in front of the church and leaned across me and Gaylord so Robbie could see it. The white family included the parents, a boy, and a girl. Behind them were a dozen dark-skinned women, each holding a smoked ham. On the opposite page was a newspaper clipping with the same picture and the headline, "Dr. Offers Holiday Cheer to Members of the Dark Race." I skimmed the article, my attention drawn to a paragraph that I read out loud:

"Dr. Nichols reasserted that the goal of racial purity was good for both races and did not require that the races be unfriendly or unkind to one another. "'The inferiority of the black race will one day be eliminated by the application of the scientific principles of eugenics,' promised Dr. Nichols. 'Equality can be achieved, however, only by diligent adherence to those principles which are now supported by the rule of law.'"

"What he was really saying is that the black race should be eliminated altogether," said Gaylord.

I handed Gaylord the photo of Doc sitting with the young woman at the poor farm.

"That sure could be Abigail Nichols," he said, "but then most white folks look alike."

The comment sent Robbie into a fit of snickering, which drew a puzzled look from Gaylord. He pointed to the family portrait. "Abigail was about ten when that was taken. She used to come to the services and sit in the back. Her brother, Willet, would come and drag her out and give her a good shaking because she hung out with those he called 'the nigger children.' Willet was full of himself before the war. The war changed him. Didn't make him nice exactly, just less mean. I think he had mental problems then, but that's just a rumor."

"And Abigail?" asked Robbie.

"Oh, that girl would take what her brother dished out and come again and again to listen to the preaching and the music. When someone got sick, she would sometimes come and help out."

"Why didn't they go to the hospital?" asked Robbie.

"Some did, but others were afraid. Like I said, there were stories about what the doctor and staff did to black people that scared off a lot of the locals."

"Like what?" I asked.

"You folks seem awfully curious about what went on at the old hospital," said Gaylord. "What's any of this got to do with the death of some old white woman?"

Gaylord's question surprised me. I was searching for an answer when Kyle came to my rescue.

"It's not them," he said, "but their client. Them being lawyers, if they don't ask all of these questions, the client will just send them back. That's how the law business works."

Kyle, now the expert on the mechanics of the legal profession, smiled proudly at Robbie and me.

Gaylord grunted dismissively. "You seem like pretty nice folks to be in such a stupid business." He cleared his throat and said, "Mothers could hear their babies crying, but were told the babies had been born dead. Some of the women who went to the hospital for minor problems were sterilized. Same for some of the men. They'd be told that they found a tumor or something and the surgery was needed to save them from dying of cancer and such. Most of the people who went to the hospital were fine. But once in a while, someone didn't come out as good as they went in."

Gaylord removed his glasses and rubbed his eyes. "Colored folk didn't like the hospital or Dr. Nichols, but everyone loved Miss Abigail. She was an angel from Heaven itself. When she was in high school, she'd come and help a dozen or so kids with their schooling. No one asked her to, and I'm sure her daddy didn't like it one bit. One day, a young girl named Dora asked her why white people were mean to black people. You have to know that we were all taught not to sass a white person, 'specially one with a mean daddy. The rest of us sort of hunkered down waiting for the young girl to receive a tongue lashing. God as my savior, I can still hear Abigail's answer. 'Because they are ignorant, Dora. Because they are afraid of people who look different.'

"She motioned Dora to her and held both of her hands. Abigail had hands the color of milk, and Dora's hands were a deep chestnut brown. Abigail looked at her, but she spoke to us. 'White people will tell you that they are better than you. Others will tell you to remember your place. Let them say what they want. Try not to hate them for it, but don't ever believe them. You can be what you want to be. It will be harder for you than it should. But don't ever quit. If I can, I'll help you.'

"She then looked at all of us and asked us to promise that we'd never accept what might be said by stupid people, no matter what color they was. I would have promised to eat glass. I'd never heard a white person say such things. She came back from college and kept at us. I think she helped pay for books and tuition for some of the kids. Anyway, from that group, I think we had three doctors, a lawyer, an engineer, and several teachers." He sighed. "She changed lives."

Though I am generally pretty good at controlling my emotions, I've acquired a sensitivity to situations in which a person is overtly kind to an animal or to another human being. Gaylord's story about Abigail was one of those situations, and I coughed to buy enough time to maintain the appearance of indifference.

"When was the last time you saw her?" I asked.

Gaylord seemed to shrivel under the weight of the question. "She came to me to help her give a black baby back to its parents. She didn't tell me how she got that baby, but I knew it was stolen. I was only twenty-one. I didn't know anything about babies. I just didn't want to go to jail for messing with a white woman and a hospital run by white people. I felt bad because she'd never asked for anything, but I said no. I started crying and wailing. Miss Abigail just hugged me and told me it was alright, that she understood. That was the last I saw of her."

"Did she say why someone would steal a baby?" asked Kyle.

"The baby was light-skinned. I mean really light. Rumor was that babies that could pass for white were killed."

I heard Robbie gasp.

"I don't know if that was true," continued Gaylord, "but I used to walk the hospital grounds over by the creek and find small bones. They're in a box under the pulpit. You can take them if you want. If Miss Abigail took that baby, it was because she was trying to do the right thing. That she was."

Gaylord grabbed the back of the bench in front of him and pulled himself up. "I can't talk about this anymore," he said.

We helped him out of the pew. He hesitated, then said, "You asked about that tall monument. The records of the cemetery are in the binder there. The burial sites were laid out in a grid, and the name of the person who was buried in a particular plot was written in the block. Many people couldn't afford stones, so keeping a record was important in those days."

I opened the binder and found yellowed and brittle papers sandwiched between plastic sleeves.

"As the remaining slaves died, burials peeked around 1910. After 1920, two or three years might elapse before another grave was dug. Another group of funerals occurred during World War II. That marker you asked about is the grave of Dorothy Lakeland."

Robbie looked at Gaylord. "Was she someone famous?"

"Not in the least. For one, she was buried here in 1944. The monument was erected almost twenty years later by an anonymous donor. There's a letter from a lawyer dated 1962 advising the church pastor that if he would allow the monument to be installed, the church would receive a gift of one thousand dollars. That was a lot of money, but folks who had relatives buried here were none too happy about having a grave marked with marble while only a few could even afford small stones. Still, the church needed the money."

Gaylord flipped to the back of the binder. "Here's the receipt from the stone carver. I called him, and he said a guy came in and paid cash. No one around here knew Dorothy, so it caused quite a stir. And the inscription didn't help. 'May you never forgive those who should have known better.' That makes it sound like folks here were mean to her, which wasn't fair because we didn't even know her. From what I heard, she was in an accident that injured her head. She died at Sweetwater Hospital. Nothing much else to tell."

"Thank you for spending the time to meet with us," said Robbie.

"Yes," said Kyle. "I guess I should be getting back to work."

I wasn't ready to leave Sweetwater, but I needed a pretext to stay. I pretended to study the receipt for a moment. "Anyone still around who might have known Dorothy as a patient?"

Robbie gave me a questioning look, which I ignored.

"I doubt she's connected to our investigation, but our client's going to see her name in our report. I don't want to have to tell him that we didn't bother asking about her."

A hint of a smile softened Gaylord's face. He looked at Kyle, who immediately closed his eyes and gritted his teeth.

"Emma Forte might remember," said Gaylord, now in full grin.

Kyle's reaction was a loud sigh and a question: "Have you seen her lately?"

Gaylord grabbed Kyle's shoulder. "The last I saw her, she was complaining about God. I think you were second. Maybe it was a draw. Anyway, I'm too old to be this cold for this long. I need to get home, pee and drink something warm."

"Let me drive you," I said.

"No need," he said. "You can look at the pictures if you want. Just set the album under the pulpit. Blow out the candles and set the lock when you leave." He tapped his way out the front door, leaving Robbie and me to stare at Kyle.

"I know what you want, but don't bother asking," said Kyle.

"We won't know if Dorothy is connected to our case unless we talk to Emma," I said. "And if we don't do it now, our client will just send us back some other time."

"Okay, okay," said Kyle raising his hands. "Just remind me on your way out of town to keep my nose out of other folk's business."

CHAPTER 9
Thursday, February 14

In the brief time we'd been with Kyle, I had him pegged as unruffable. But the prospect of meeting with Emma Forte had sent him into thinking and rethinking how he would approach her. He didn't share any reasons for his trepidation, but his apprehension was contagious, and soon Robbie was wondering out loud whether visiting her was worth all the anxiety.

"She's going to expect something in return for answering your questions," said Kyle.

"Like what?" I asked.

"Emma has a taste for good liquor," he replied. "I have an unopened bottle of Glenlivet Nadurra Oloroso single malt scotch, but it's going to cost you a hundred dollars. I'm not sure that the Glenlivet will satisfy her, but that's all I have."

Emma lived in a house just south of Main Street, where she had been employed by Kyle as a "security officer" for the past five years. Previously, she'd lived in a small cabin with her husband on one of the hills surrounding Sweetwater. With his death and her advancing years, she was unable to manage for herself. Kyle had tried to assist her in her home, but, as he put it, "her needs outstripped my patience." Apparently, not much had changed on that score in five years, hence his reluctance to initiate a visit.

Emma's house was a small Cape Cod, painted a soft cream yellow with white window trim and dark shutters. A porch stretched across the front of the house, providing a place to sit in the summer and to store firewood in the winter. The pathway to the door had been freshly shoveled and salted, a task I assumed had been performed by Kyle while Emma slept.

We knocked on the front door and waited. A moment later, an elderly black woman in a gray sweater and wool pants appeared in the doorway. She stood silently, her attention shifting from Robbie to me. With a glance at Kyle, she turned her back and said, "For the love of God, come in and shut the door."

We followed her into a living room brightly lit by a large bay window. The windowsill was occupied by an orange tabby cat basking in a sunbeam, a paw draped over its eyes. In the middle of the room was a sofa flanked by reclining chairs that faced a large television. Emma dropped herself into one of the recliners and turned the TV on. "So, who are you two? If you're Jehovah's witnesses, save your breath. I'm not happy with God right now and He's obviously got a bone to pick with me. No amount of scripture is going to make it better."

The television came on with a loud hiss. The picture was a jumble of white and black dots. "That's all I get. Damn thing never works and Kyle never comes to fix it."

"It's not broken," said Kyle patiently. "You've just used the wrong remote and changed the channel from three to four again." He took the remote from her hand and pressed a button. We were momentarily blasted by the voice of a young, shapely woman talking about a car before Kyle managed to turn down the volume.

"I got two hundred channels and nothing worth watching," snapped Emma. She turned the television off and focused on us. "Two young white folks don't come to an old colored woman's house without having a reason, and if that reason doesn't include fixing all that's broken around here, don't bother getting comfortable." She looked again at me. "What's in the bag?"

"We understand that you used to work at the hospital," I said.

Emma folded her arms across her chest. "Why would that be any business of yours?"

"They have a few questions about a woman named Dorothy Lakeland," said Kyle. Emma had perfected the expressionless stare of a poker player and would have been able to convincingly deny ever having heard the name but for the tightening of her hands around her arms.

In my chair across from her, I removed the bottle of scotch from the bag and handed it to her. She took it reluctantly. "You must have something powerfully unpleasant on your mind to be offering a bottle of Glenlivet. Not that I'm accepting it."

"An elderly woman was beaten to death a few weeks ago," I said. "We're exploring a possible connection between the victim, Abigail Nichols, and Sweetwater Hospital. For reasons I'm not at liberty to disclose, there might also be a connection to Dorothy Lakeland. We were hoping you could help us."

I had no idea what that connection might be and was relieved when Emma didn't ask.

Emma closed her eyes and lowered her head. "Mercy, mercy. An old woman murdered? I don't know what Abigail could have to do with any of that. That sweet girl had no business being born into that family of low-lifes. Life is hard enough, but some folks seem hell-bent on making it worse." She examined the bottle of scotch and sighed. "I can see you won't be leaving until you get what you came for, so for God's sakes, take off your coats. Now, if I'm going to talk about Sweetwater, I'm going to need a taste." She glanced at Kyle. "I like it on the rocks. I'll start with two fingers."

Robbie sat on the sofa closest to Emma. Kyle returned with a glass full of ice, then broke the seal on the bottle and poured until Emma signaled that the glass was full enough. She sipped the scotch and smiled. "My daddy was a waiter at the hospital," she said. "Most people don't know that it was like a country club for the white doctors. Black men wearing white gloves waited on those miserable men and bowed to them like they was gods. Now my daddy made some of the best apple brandy you ever tasted. Once, he got busted by some federal agents, but the judge and the prosecutor drank all the evidence before the trial and later asked Daddy for a little more. Willet and Dr. Nichols had a liking for it. Daddy would trade a little bottle of that brandy for partial bottles of wine and spirits. When we got older, Daddy'd give us a taste, then explain how each was made and why some was better than others. He sure knew his stuff."

We all waited while Emma sipped her drink and traveled back in time. Judging from the audible sighs and the flashes of sadness that crossed her face, the journey was a difficult and painful one. She started to speak a few times, only to moan softly instead.

After a few minutes, she said, "I graduated from nursing school in January of 1942 and went to work at Sweetwater a few weeks later. We was trained to help the sick, but for black nurses at white hospitals, most of the work was changing bed pans, bathing patients, and making beds. Sweetwater had a black wing where the black nurses also cared for the patients. So it was a good job at a time when having a job was a godsend. Patients came and went, mostly like any other hospital. But some patients…"

Emma took a generous drink and closed her eyes.

"Dorothy Lakeland was a young black woman who was admitted in 1939. A farm machine had thrown a metal rod that penetrated her skull. She was brain dead but otherwise healthy. Occasionally, black nurses would be detailed to the white wing. We weren't allowed above the third floor. I went to the fourth floor by mistake and discovered Dorothy in a nice room. She looked to be about eight months pregnant. A white nurse found me and screamed at me to leave at once. Later, Dr. Nichols came to explain that Dorothy was a special case, that things weren't what they looked like, and that it was important that I forget what I'd seen."

"She'd been raped?" asked Robbie.

Emma grimaced. "Yes, but not in the way you was thinking. I couldn't stop thinking about her. So about six months later, I went back. I waited for two nurses to leave her room, and looked in. She was just starting to show that she was pregnant again."

"I don't understand," said Kyle.

"You will if you just sit and listen," snapped Emma. "I wasn't the only nurse to stumble in on Dorothy, so at breaks, I started to act like I knew everything. You know, like 'I see the Lakeland woman's pregnant again' and waited to see if anyone would say anything. Nobody did, but I could see that an older nurse was hiding some information. She was ailing with arthritis and couldn't always finish folding her sheets and towels, so I would do it for her. One day, I asked her point blank about Dorothy, and she tells me Dorothy's been pregnant at least a half dozen times. One of the doctors would examine the baby, write notes about it in a book, and then sometime later, Dorothy would be pregnant again. I asked her about the babies, but she just said, 'What do you think happened to them?' God's been punishing me ever since for not doing something to help that poor woman. I guess He got tired of waiting for me because He took her away from that hell hole a few years later. She's buried in the church cemetery under that God awful marble tower."

Emma's story left us sharing an uneasy silence. Whatever I expected Dorothy's story to be, the one told by Emma was not it.

"Any idea who the father was?" asked Robbie.

"Yes I do. Willet Nichols fathered at least a few of those babies. Now, before you get to thinking he was some kind of animal, the idea of him laying with Dorothy came from his daddy, Dr. Nichols. I saw Willet some times while this was going on, and he didn't look right to me. If it weren't such a terrible thing they was doing to Dorothy, I might have felt sorry for him. I think he was relieved when she died. We all were."

"Do you know where Willet is now?" I asked.

Emma glanced at Kyle. "No. I see him around sometimes, but I couldn't tell you where he is."

"What do you know about Abigail Nichols taking a black baby?" asked Robbie.

Emma drained her glass. "Lordy. Lawyers are worse than missionaries. If I'm going have to answer more questions, somebody better put fresh ice in my glass and fill it again."

Kyle complied with the request and Emma leaned back in her chair. Whether it was the alcohol or the relief of unburdening her conscience, Emma no longer seemed frightened by her memories.

"I got to know Abigail at church. One day in the spring of 1943, when

I'd say she was about nineteen, she was in the chapel sobbing. She told me she'd read articles written by Dr. Nichols, her father, about keeping the white race white. Worse, she'd read a letter from a Nazi scientist thanking her father for all his help removing misfits and undesirables from the world population. She'd heard rumors about experiments being conducted at Sweetwater and wondered aloud if she should shoot him. I told her she shouldn't, but I confess I thought otherwise. Over the years, I chatted with her whenever she'd come to town. She traveled a lot, and she came to church to tell stories about places she'd been. The stories about the concentration camps were hard to listen to, but she'd tell 'em just like she talked about going to Tahiti.

"In 1953, her father was in his sixties and in poor health. Willet was in and out of the ward for mentally ill patients. The hospital was in the hands of a man whose name I can't remember. Because of rumors about the goings-on at the hospital, black women tried to avoid coming to Sweetwater to give birth, but many had no place else to go. I was in the maternity ward of the hospital's black wing one day when I heard a white doctor talking to a nurse about a newborn baby being 'too white' and agreeing that the boy might 'pass' when he got older. They agreed to report the baby's death as 'due to heart issues' and to 'take care of the mother and father.' I stole that baby and called Abigail. She told me that I'd done the right thing, but it didn't feel that way to me. Nobody called the cops. The baby was reported dead. The mother was sterilized before she was discharged. The father was told that the birth defect was his fault and he needed to be examined. They told him he had a growth that needed to be removed, and then they sterilized him."

"So what did Abigail do with the baby?" asked Robbie.

"She found out who his parents was and tried to return him, but they thought she was playing a cruel joke. I was afraid I would be arrested for kidnapping or that the baby would die. But Abigail told me not to worry. She said something about her father's papers protecting her and the baby. I didn't think to ask what she meant, but that was the last I ever saw of her."

"Did she say where the papers were?" asked Kyle.

"I said I didn't ask!" snapped Emma.

What energy she had left drained from Emma's face. She lowered her head and stared into her half empty glass. "God has never forgiven me for stealing that baby, for taking it from his mother. He never will."

Gone was the bravado with which Emma had greeted us an hour earlier. The Emma before us was tired and lonely, with only her memories for company. She was a ghost in a ghost town, a prisoner of a dead town buried in a seemingly endless winter. The days were as still as the nights, fertile grounds for haunting by the voices of guilt and regret that had taken refuge in the spaces where hope had once lived. The snow would melt, the green and color of spring would return, and these voices would be tamped down. But from the perspective of the moment, that reality was a dim light at the end of a long dark tunnel. I searched for words to comfort her, but none came to mind.

Kyle and I took care of a few minor repairs, replacing a few light bulbs and tightening a nut on a leaky faucet. As we put on our coats, I turned to her and asked: "Do you remember the name of the parents of that baby?"

Emma nodded. "What I remember is the name given to that baby, John Mason Laggard. Big name for a newborn baby. I think about him every day."

The name "Mason" should have come as no surprise. Still, confirmation of the kidnapping left me staring at Emma. Stories about the cruelty with which white men treated minorities produce an intellectual outrage rooted in a sense of fairness. But the pain and suffering is difficult to grasp even for the most empathetic listener. Hearing the name John Mason Laggard, I saw the events through Reggie's eyes. Baby John's fate was determined solely by the color of his skin. He was simply not black enough. Hard as I tried, I couldn't fathom how anyone could think that way. How, I wondered, could anyone taught to heal and comfort other human beings murder an innocent baby?

My reaction apparently frightened Emma. "I don't know what I said," she said to Kyle.

I forced a smile and apologized. "I'm so sorry, Emma. I just thought for a moment that I knew someone by that name. Please forgive me."

We left Emma with her memories and her scotch. It was nearly two when we got back to the police station. Robbie was keen on getting back to Lyle before dark, but Kyle was insistent on feeding us leftovers and coffee. As we left Sweetwater, Robbie turned and looked at me.

"What?" I said, somewhat defensively.

"What I heard today was gut wrenching. But I have to admit I see why you do this. I mean, despite what we learned, I thought today was awesome. I know that sounds cold, but I don't mean it that way. Hearing what happened here was intoxicating. I want to talk to Willet and Baby John and the woman who took care of Ruth. I want to know about the papers Abigail stole and why she thought they'd protect her. I just want to do it now. Do you understand that?"

I did and I said so. What I didn't say was that what had started out as an inquiry about the fate of Reggie's cousin had become something larger. How many children had suffered the fate intended for Baby John? How many men and women had been sterilized without their knowledge and consent? And more to the point, what could I do about it all these many years later?

———————

I dropped Robbie off at her house just as the sun was setting. We were pretty much talked out. A quick peck on the cheek and she was out of the car.

When I arrived at the farm, I was greeted with a note from Markus and two very cold and unhappy cats. The note was brief but to the point: "Filled oil tank. Relit burner. Your big cat and the one who lost his ear ran out the door. Sorry. Markus."

Rocky and Van Gogh rushed into a very toasty house and were greeted by Molly and Atisha, the two smarter felines who had stayed inside and eaten most of the day. I refilled their bowls while listening to my messages.

Robbie's voice was tired and stressed. "Check your voicemail. The IRS agent is coming tomorrow to discuss the tax issues with Reilly's estate. I hope you're ready." The next message was from an Agent Felix Bauer. "Mr. Harrington. I have attempted many times to communicate with you regarding the tax issues with the estate of Reilly Heartwood. I will be at your home in Lyle tomorrow morning and expect you to be there. This is my last polite request."

Agent Bauer's frustration with me was certainly justified. I had received letters and phone messages last fall requesting I call him. Unfortunately, the timing of his requests coincided with a battle with pain pills. I was inadvertently instructed to take twice the prescribed dose. The error took a while to figure out, and, by that time, I was addicted. Coming off the pills was a lot harder than getting on them. For a few months, I ignored the mail and anything else that required concentration. Robbie helped pay my bills and intervened to smooth things over with Agent Bauer. She set up a meeting with Agent Bauer for March first. What had caused him to accelerate his visit and to issue what amounted to a threat was worrisome.

I mustered the energy to call Gus. I brought him up to speed on what I knew about Abigail Nichols and summarized my visit to Sweetwater. To my relief, Gus spared me a lecture on the risks of my trip to Sweetwater, and asked only what he could do for me. We agreed that he would research the Anderson Historical Foundation, and find out who actually funded the purchase of the Sweetwater Hospital and the Nichols residence.

I thought about calling Reggie but heated a cup of cider, added a splash of rum, and took a seat on the porch of the old house instead. The air was still and cold, the sky clear and deeply black. Stars pricked holes in the black dome, sending ancient light from distances that were incomprehensible. Still, I stared at them, wondering, as humans have wondered for eons, what it all meant. With the vastness of the universe as a reference, I supposed that nothing I did or thought mattered very much. But I lived in a small space with other humans where trivial things like skin color mattered a great deal. For a species that revels in its intellectual and moral sophistication, I simply couldn't grasp why we treat each other with such cruelty. I thought of the box of small bones I'd taken from the church and again wondered how anyone could murder a child.

I sighed away thoughts that were just too heavy to contemplate. I drank my cider and refused to think any more about Abigail Nichols, John Mason Laggard, or Dorothy Lakeland. Tomorrow, I would play my part in the human drama. I would discuss taxes and deal with Reggie. I would care about who killed Abigail. But for this brief moment, staring into eternity, I found peace in the realization that in a larger context, what I did, said, and thought really didn't matter.

CHAPTER 10
Friday, February 15

I arrived at Heartwood House at a time I thought was early, only to see a small BMW with DC plates parked next to Robbie's SUV in the driveway. I stepped from my car into brilliant sunshine. The air was warm and heavy with the smell of melting snow and ice. The pinging of water dripping from gutters and roofs announced that a thaw was underway. It raised the hope that we would soon be released from our prison of snow and cold. On another day, I might have taken a moment to revel in this reminder that winter was not a permanent state, but today was all about taxes and money.

In the foyer, I was greeted by the aromas of breakfast and the sound of voices emanating from the kitchen. When I appeared, the conversation continued unabated. The center of attention was a short bulldog of a man eating from a plate of hotcakes and bacon while trying to listen to Carrie and Cecil simultaneously. After a moment, Carrie turned and smiled at me.

"This is Agent Felix Bauer," she said. "He's come all the way from Washington to talk to you about taxes you didn't pay. I think he's a nice man and you should pay him what he says you owe him."

"Well then, that settles that," I said. I ignored a smirk from Robbie and poured a cup of coffee.

"Carrie, Cecil, and Harry have been telling me how they came to live here," said Agent Bauer. "They said it was your idea."

"I wanted them to be closer to town, where they could be around other folks and have access to medical attention should they need it," I said. "I live on the farm where I can avoid other folks and most of what passes as civilization. So it works for everyone."

"After prison, I guess solitude must feel like a luxury," replied the agent.

"Something like that."

Lora Jean Brady appeared in the kitchen, looked at the group of adults, and expressed her annoyance with an aggrieved-teenager smile. LJ had been a part-time resident of Heartwood House before Reilly's death. Her father was in prison for bank robbery. LJ's mother, Beth, spent a year in a court-ordered treatment center for drug addiction. She was released last September and arrested in October for trafficking in cocaine. It was clear to everyone that she was a mule, carrying packages of drugs to earn money that supported her habit. Even the judge recognized that Beth was sick and needed help, not confinement. But the politicians have hijacked the justice system to satisfy a political objective—to appear tough on criminals. Beth's offense carried a mandatory sentence of ten years, and the judge had no power to consider any mitigating circumstances. Reluctantly, he ordered her to prison, where the state would care for her at taxpayer's expense. A corporation operated the prison where Beth would serve her sentence. It just so happened to be the same corporation that lobbied hard for the mandatory sentencing laws. Capitalism had triumphed over justice, but now we could at least feel safe that Beth was no longer wreaking havoc in our streets.

All of this made LJ a stoic seventeen-year-old. She was also pretty, smart, and confident. LJ had handled her mother's situation well, almost as if she'd expected her mother to fail. LJ, I was certain, would not fall into the traps of her parents.

"And who may you be?" asked Agent Bauer.

Frieda introduced LJ, then insisted she join the table for breakfast. "No time," she said. "I don't want to be late." She snatched a strip of bacon from a plate, offered a perfunctory "bye," and dashed from the kitchen.

Agent Bauer stood up and complimented Frieda for a wonderful breakfast, then looked at me. "Is there some place where we can talk?"

The question and the tone in which it was asked quieted the room. The joy of the previous moments evaporated as smiles were replaced by worry lines and furrows. I led the agent and Robbie through the living room to the study. The agent hesitated at the study door, his attention focused on the living room. After a few moments, he seemed to bow his head and nod before following me into the room that once was Reilly's office. I had barely shut the door before he started speaking.

"I have prepared a complaint accusing you of various counts of tax evasion, willful failure to pay taxes, willful failure to file a return, interference with the administration of the tax laws, and conspiracy. Add all the counts together and you could be sent to prison for a long time. The complaint asks that all your assets and the assets of Reilly's estate be frozen. If you want to scream and holler, then I'll make a call and the complaint will be filed. If you would like to talk to me in a civil tone, I might be amenable to hearing your side of the issue before I make up my mind about filing the complaint."

"I'm more than willing to be civil," I said.

Robbie and I sat across from him. He studied us, then opened his briefcase. "Just so you understand the seriousness of this matter, I have a listing of the numerous tax code violations you've committed and the possible penalties you face." For a moment, his face was obscured by the top of the briefcase. I heard papers rustling followed by a loud sigh. Then, I heard his weary voice: "No. I can't do this."

He slammed the case shut. Agent Bauer reappeared, his arms folded across his chest, exhaustion written on his face. "I'm too old to play the bad guy. I don't want to threaten you. But I've been writing you for months asking you to contact me so we can straighten out this mess before I retire. By not responding, you look guilty."

"Yes sir," I said. "I kind of checked out for a while. I'm sorry. I'm better now."

"Yes. Robbie explained all that over breakfast. Still, we need to fix this before I lose control of the case. I'm retiring soon, so there's not much time. My replacement is a young man eager to prove himself. He hasn't gotten wind of this just yet, but if he does, he'll drain every penny from Mr. Heartwood's estate and come after you. This case would make him a rising star."

"How bad is it?" I asked.

"It's not just the taxes but the penalties. About $750,000. Of course, my replacement will dig deeper. Who knows what he'll find."

The number seemed to hang in the room.

"Young guys love to bring criminal charges, so keep that in mind as you consider your response."

"So we pay that and we're clear?" I asked.

"That's a lot of money," cautioned Robbie.

Agent Bauer nodded, but his thoughts seemed elsewhere. "I was a big fan of Reilly Heartwood."

Reilly Heartwood recorded under the stage name CC Hollinger. Real fans knew him by both names.

"I came here for his wake," continued the Agent. "I'm not sure if we met or not."

"It was a tough day," I said.

"When my son was old enough, I took him to a concert. My son was terminally ill then and had a hard time with pain and such. Reilly heard about him from one of the ushers and gave him a backstage pass." Bauer's voice caught as the emotion of the old memory was renewed. "My son died a few months later, but he never stopped talking about the moment he spent with a famous singer. He said it was the best day of his life."

"Reilly was like that," I said, touched by the agent's grief.

"He was a great singer and human being," continued Bauer, "but he made a mess of his taxes. He's got his personal deductions mixed up with his charities. He appears to have deducted contributions that he didn't make. He's claimed deductions for charities that have had their tax status changed or revoked. But I know he meant well. He was trying to do something good. I'm comfortable believing that Reilly never intended to commit tax evasion. But I don't know you. Your conviction for fraud may have been overturned, but you put yourself in a situation that looks shady.

I want to believe that your lack of cooperation was excusable, but I don't want to be conned."

Robbie gave me a puzzled look. "I think you lost me," I said.

"I'd like to see your farm," he said standing. "We can continue our discussion there."

He left Robbie and me staring at each other.

"What's he up to?" asked Robbie. "I mean, he threatens you, then acts like he wants to help you."

"I guess we'll find out shortly."

I offered to give the agent directions to the farm, but he said he knew where it was. When I left the house, Agent Bauer was already in his car, headed down the driveway, and pursuing an agenda I didn't understand.

The poor farm was located a few miles to the north and west of Lyle. The driveway was a dirt road marked by a break in a barbed wire fence and a large rusted mailbox sitting on a post. I had replaced the post but not the old mailbox, which was still marked by faded letters announcing the fence opening as the way in to "FARM No. 38."

I caught up with Agent Bauer's car at the farm's entrance. He seemed to be studying the mailbox, but he could have just been waiting for me. He started down the driveway, his front wheels spraying his car with sheets of muddy water mixed with chunks of ice. But even the gauntlet of ruts and brown water didn't slow him.

He pulled in front of the main house and waited for me. When I got out of my car, he started to the front door.

"Wait!" I shouted before catching up with him. "This building is unsafe. I live in the bunkhouse."

"Are you saying I can't go in?" he said, his tone thick with suspicion.

I shook my head. "Not saying that. But you'll need to sign a waiver and a release first."

"I need to know if you are concealing property, Mr. Harrington. I'll take my chances."

"All right. We have to leave the front door open, and if the house creaks once, we're done."

The inspection of the house took only a few minutes. The agent peered into the two lower bedrooms and opened a few closets. When he entered the kitchen and saw the sloping floor, he quickly lost interest in any further inspection.

I took him to the bunkhouse and let him wander. The cats followed him but he ignored them.

I offered him coffee. When I returned from the kitchen with two cups, he was sitting at the café table flipping through the pages of a picture album.

"Who is this?" he asked.

He held up the album and pointed to a photo of me as a teenager helping a man move a large boulder from a field. I was filling out my tall frame and enjoying the strength of new muscles. A second picture showed the two of us in weight-lifter poses. The man's face was painted with the same childish smile as mine. I removed the picture from the album and flipped it over. "1986 – Col. Simon Raker (RET) 63; purple heart (Guadalcanal) with Shep 16."

"You seemed to have been friendly with the people who came here"

"I was just a kid. I didn't know what this place was or who these people were. They were nice to me and I was nice to them. If you're asking if I looked down on them, no, I didn't."

Agent Bauer alternated looking at the picture and looking at the inscription on the back. I could hear him sighing softly. After a few moments, he said, "When Simon was a little older than you, he was fighting the Japanese in the Pacific. When you met him, he was a decorated war veteran living out his life moving rocks for a few square meals and a bed. Doesn't seem right."

It didn't, but I needed Agent Bauer to focus on the problem at hand. "You've seen Heartwood House. You've seen the farm. Why don't you tell me what it is you want me to do?"

Agent Bauer leaned over the table. "Reilly's estate owes a lot of money. If I were dealing with him, I'd tell him that he'll have to pay what he owes and the penalties that have accrued. After the kindness he showed my son, I'd be willing to help him with refiling his returns and looking for ways to actually reduce the taxes he owes. You see what I'm saying? But of course I'm not talking to him, I'm talking to you. I'm trying to find a way to trust you. What I've seen tells me that you have a generous side. I don't see that you've spent a lot on yourself. But you have a history that's not reassuring. You can understand why I'm skeptical about your intentions."

The truth was that I had no intentions. Reilly's money and his other assets were supposedly mine, but I had yet to embrace the idea. Agent Bauer sensed my indecision and tried to reassure me.

"You don't have to say anything, Mr. Harrington. I know a tax attorney who will look over the filings for you and prepare the necessary amendments. She's very good and may find ways of reducing the estate's tax liability. If you were to refile all of Reilly's personal returns for the past five years, and all of the returns for a dozen or so charities, and pay back the taxes owed and the penalty, that would fix it. Just keep in mind that in two months, I will be gone and you will need to deal with someone new."

I shook my head. "I want this to go away."

Agent Bauer looked at me. "You remind me of Reilly. He was impatient to fix things. I think we can resolve this quickly, but you have to communicate with me. You don't want to go back to prison, and God knows I don't want to send you there."

"No, I certainly don't. Thank you."

I walked Agent Bauer to his car. The meeting buoyed my spirits. I was about to thank him again when a police cruiser pulled up in front of us. Reggie lifted his huge frame from his car with amazing agility and walked quickly toward me.

He nodded at Agent Bauer, then looked me in the eye. "I've been trying to reach you all morning. Some reason you're not taking my calls?" He spoke calmly but he stood rigidly, his eyes revealing an uncharacteristic edginess.

Both Reggie and I towered over Felix Bauer. Reggie's bear-like frame and his expression made the agent take a step back.

"Reggie, this is Agent Bauer from the IRS…"

"Nice to meet you, sir. I'm afraid I have something I need to discuss with Mr. Harrington in private."

"If you wait just a few minutes, I'll be right with you."

"Well, you know I have been waiting, and I really need to speak with you now. Right now."

I became aware without even looking that Agent Bauer had heard enough. A car door slammed and tires spun in the mud. He was gone.

If Reggie said anything else, I didn't hear it. Instead, I heard my own voice, thick with frustration, "For God's sake, Reggie…I'm sorry. I should have called, but things got crazy busy. I learned some things about your cousin. I didn't find him, but I think I can track him down. Happy now?"

"I just thought you might have called or something."

"And you could have been more patient. You may have just gotten me indicted for tax fraud. So pardon me if I'm not happy to see you."

"And how did I do that?"

"Reilly's estate is in the hole for $750,000 of back taxes and penalties. Agent Bauer was trying to determine whether to believe that my failure to respond to his letters wasn't willful evasion. Instead of making nice with the tax man, I engaged in a shouting match with a crazed cop. So, I think we can conclude it didn't go too well with Agent Bauer."

Reggie gave me a contrite look. "That number's gonna make me feel bad for a long time. I could call him and say I was sorry, and out of line, even tell him how you've been really good to me and all."

"Probably best that we not go there."

"Can I ask you about Baby John now, or are you still pissed?"

I exhaled loudly and shrugged. "What's a few hundred grand among friends? You know I can't stay pissed at you for very long. Anyway, the tax guy should grow some cojones and develop a sense of humor."

I walked to the porch of the old farm house and took a seat in an old rocking chair. Reggie joined me, and I proceeded to give him a detailed explanation of my trip to Sweetwater and conversations with Gaylord Macklin and Emma Forte.

"It was hard enough to learn that Baby John is still alive," he said. "But you pretty much confirmed what my Aunt Betty told me. I have to admit, I didn't buy the whole story about him being stolen, but that's what happened. Killing babies because they weren't black enough? Now that's hard to get your head wrapped around, but I've seen white folks do some pretty nasty stuff."

"It's possible that Abigail Nichols took care of him and he learned to care about her," I said.

"It's also possible that when he grew older, he resented her for taking him away from his family. So, with him being alive and having a possible motive, there's a chance that Albert might not be guilty after all. As I said when I came to your office, I'd have a hard time living with that." Reggie laughed. "Keeping from Detective Hunter what I know about Baby John is probably worth two more felony counts."

After a moment, he faced me and said, "You know this isn't about me anymore, right? You realize what happened to my family is only the tip of the iceberg, okay? How many others suffered the same fates? The people who did this have gotten away with it for fifty years. I can't let this lie."

"Yeah. The same thought occurred to me as well. Do you have the case file in your car?"

Reggie nodded. "I have what my friend could copy without attracting attention. But this isn't your fight." Reggie stood up. "I'll handle it from here on. I want you to drop it."

"Really? You want me to forget what I heard, and go on doing whatever it is I do? Yeah, well, that's not going to happen. So cut the crap and get the file. Let's take a look and see what we can come up with."

CHAPTER 11
Friday, February 15

Reggie and I sat at the café table in the bunkhouse and reviewed the case file of Abigail Nichols' murder. He handed me an eight-by-ten photo taken in her living room. A pool of blood darkened the floor. Blood was splattered on the wall and the furniture. When I looked up, he handed me a second picture of the victim draped across a bed. The picture was taken from a distance, but the damage to her face was still easily discernible. He handed me another picture and said, "This is what she looked like before she was attacked."

I handed Reggie the photograph of Abigail Nichols taken by Harry. "I don't know if it's any consolation, but your cousin couldn't have been raised by a kinder person," I said.

"He should have been raised by his momma and papa," said Reggie. "Knowing the pain his kidnapping caused my aunt and uncle and still causes my family, it wouldn't matter to me if she was Mother Teresa."

I didn't press the point any further. "So, someone beats her and then carries her to her bedroom?"

Reggie nodded. "That's what Detective Hunter believes happened."

I looked again at the picture of Abigail lying on the bed. "Give me a reason to believe that Albert Loftus did this?"

"The prevailing theory is that Albert believed Jennifer Rice was hiding money in the house and kept hitting her to get her to talk. Basically, he just got carried away."

"And the cops focused on Albert because of an anonymous tip?"

"A guy called and said he saw a man running out of the house and jumping into a truck. He gave a partial plate number and hung up. A neighbor told police that he thought he saw someone come out of the garage door. He didn't see where the man went, but he confirmed that a truck parked in front of the driveway was driven away shortly after he saw the man come out of the garage door. Not exactly consistent but close enough. They caught up with Albert trying to leave town."

I studied the two photos. "I was in a minimum security facility with lots of white collar criminals. Most of these guys were wimps, afraid of the shadows, afraid to sit too long on the toilet, afraid of sleeping at night. But not all were like that. Sometimes a prosecutor would trade time in a minimum security prison for information, so we had a few thugs in our midst. An inmate named Carlos was an accountant accused of stealing money from his employer. Rumor was that he had a stash of cash. Three tough guys were getting out and wanted Carlos to tell them where the money was. He wouldn't or couldn't. The beating was methodical and slow. His fingers were broken. Most of his teeth were knocked out or broken. When it was done, Carlos was brain dead. Abigail doesn't look to have been tortured, just beaten."

"So what's your point? Albert wanted to know where her money was. He hit her too hard, thought bad about it, and put her in her bed thinking she was still alive. Case still closed."

"Show me the close-ups of her face and hands"

"You sure?" asked Reggie.

I nodded and understood why he'd asked. Abigail's left eye had been punctured and her nose bent to a horrific angle. But for all the gore, the photographs offered an alternate theory of why she was beaten. I pointed to her hand. "Tell me that someone intent on stealing money would have left what looks like a two-carat diamond ring on her finger? Even if it isn't real, it looks like it might be." I showed Reggie the photo of the living room. "That's a diamond stud earring next to the chair leg. Why didn't Albert pick it up?"

"The facts never line up perfectly. Albert admits to being at the scene, and there were stolen items in his car. Those are pretty solid reasons to accuse him of murder. There is no evidence that, as he claims, he was framed. For Albert's story to be true, the actual killer would have had to be in the house when he arrived, avoided being seen, and taken the jewelry to Albert's truck before he got there. Albert said he came in, saw the body, and left. You have to go where the facts take you, even if your gut says something's not right."

"All right. Now tell me why we should think that Albert didn't kill her."

Reggie handed me two DNA reports. "This sample is from a cup found on the kitchen counter. It's a partial match to the victim. It's probable that it belongs to a sibling of the victim. Keep in mind that for now, the police believe that the victim is Jennifer Rice. She didn't have any known siblings, so the DNA evidence is considered inconclusive. Abigail Nichols, on the other hand, has a brother, Willet, and it's likely that the DNA came from him.

"The other report is from a sample taken from a glass in the dishwasher. That sample belongs to Baby John. Again, my uncle isn't known to have any children. We also know that violence is not something that Albert is known for. The DNA doesn't prove anything because we have no way of knowing when the cup and glass were used. But just the fact that Willet and Baby John knew the victim well enough to be in her house makes them persons of interest. Until Detective Hunter eliminates them as suspects, it's hard to imagine a defense attorney who couldn't convince at least one juror that Albert isn't guilty beyond a reasonable doubt. Of course, we haven't told Detective Hunter about Willet and Baby John, so she can't really do her job."

"So far, we're doing it for her," I said. "I don't see how we're impeding her investigation in any way."

Reggie grimaced. "I don't know if I can play this game, Shep. I screwed up using the DNA database for my own purposes. Now I'm keeping a colleague of mine from doing her job. What if Albert killed Abigail but the truth about who she was, and about the DNA, doesn't come out until the trial or on appeal? He'll walk and Detective Hunter's reputation will be ruined. I don't think I can keep quiet any longer."

I ignored him. "Willet has been looking for something in the old Nichols home for years, so maybe he thought his sister knew where it was. He might have asked her and, when she said she didn't know, he hit her"

"So how do you explain the stolen jewelry found in Albert's car?" asked Reggie.

"I don't know. Maybe Albert did it."

Reggie shrugged. "So basically we have no idea who killed Abigail or where Baby John is. How is all of this talk getting us anywhere?"

I retrieved two beers from the fridge and offered one to Reggie. "You know how this works. A few days ago, we didn't know whether Baby John was alive or who took him. Give me a few more days. I'll keep asking questions until something turns up."

"You keep saying that," replied Reggie. He slipped the pictures and DNA reports into the folder. "A few days and that's it."

"You hungry? Frieda left half a meat loaf and part of a German chocolate cake in the fridge."

I put the meat loaf in the microwave. Reggie stared at me across the kitchen table.

"Something you'd like to say?" I asked.

"Now that we're friends again, I think I can be honest and say, no offense intended, that it appears you've moved from one dump to another. Reilly left you a lot of money. You could afford to live better."

"Robbie, Doc, Frieda, my aunt, the cats—all want to know what I'm going to do with my life, and I give them the same answer. I don't have a clue."

Reggie scoffed. "That's bullshit. If you didn't have a clue, you would have left here after you were shot. But you didn't. So, you see, I think you do have an idea. I think something has popped into your head but you're keeping it to yourself. I want to know what it is."

I heard the microwave ding, but I didn't move. "I might have had a thought or two. So what?"

"Tell me."

"I haven't really thought it through"

"Tell me anyway."

"All right, but if I even think you're chuckling, I'll break this beer bottle over your head."

Reggie stifled a laugh. "No chuckling."

"When I was high on pain pills, I used to think about reopening the poor farm. It's crazy, but that's what's occurred to me. So, now that we're done with that, let's eat."

Reggie grabbed my arm. "That's one fucking crazy thought," he said. "I think it is like fantastically cool!"

I waved my hand at him. "It's a drug-induced fantasy."

I put the meat loaf on the table and let Reggie help himself. "So how would your poor farm actually work?" he asked. "Would you bring in the poor and the helpless and use them as free labor? You know, raise cotton, corn, and taters, like in the song?"

"I don't want to talk about it," I said defensively.

"Yup. You could be called Massa Shep. I think it suits you. You could sell Massa Shep mugs and T-shirts online."

I put down my fork. "All right, all right. Here it is. I would find people capable of sustaining themselves but who've had bad luck. A lost job. An illness. An abusive spouse. A one-time brush with the law. I'd have a training center for the adults, and a school for the kids. After training, I would help find each adult a job or help him or her start a business. For a year, I would provide them adult housing and maybe subsidize their salary. If a graduate of the program agrees to help train another person, I would help with the expenses. I'd like to build an amphitheater in the pasture so that, during the summer, we could have benefit concerts to raise money for the farm. Maybe we'd also have a music program for the kids."

Reggie stared at me for a moment, then returned to eating. "Yup. I can see you haven't thought about it much."

"Now you know."

We ate in silence. I cleared the dinner plates and offered Reggie coffee.

"What Abigail offered those kids at the church was hope," he said."Hope is a very precious thing to offer folks looking down a dark hole. I think your idea for the farm may seem way out there to some, but that's what hope is about. For all your flaws and demons, you're the most hopeful person I know. I like your idea. I think you should think it through some more, get some advice from people who know about these things, and go for it."

I brought two large slabs of cake to the table. "Jesus Christ, Reggie, you're as crazy as I am."

He laughed. "It would appear so."

Reggie left me the case file and a lot to think about. He promised that he would resist any impulse to call Detective Hunter, and I promised to keep him in the loop with whatever I learned.

With so much to think about, I was like a cat in front of a door. When inside, the cat wants out. When outside, the cat wants in. Basically, the cat wants the door to be removed so it doesn't have to decide one way or the other.

So when I was thinking about Abigail's murder, I was distracted by the idea of opening the poor farm. When I was thinking about the farm, my thoughts turned to the pictures of Abigail and the fate of Reggie's cousin. In the process, I forgot about calling Robbie, an oversight that I regretted as soon as I heard my phone ring.

"You better have a good reason for not calling," she said.

"Reggie said pretty much the same thing when I forgot to call him"

"I'm waiting."

"I'm sure I do, I just can't recall what it is at the moment"

"So did you make nice to Agent Bauer?"

"I did. I think we were on our way to being good friends when Reggie showed up. He and I kind of got into a shouting match."

"Kind of how bad?"

"You know. Two guys showing off their muscles, talking loud, and spraying spittle at each other."

"And Agent Bauer witnessed this confrontation?"

"Some of it. I think he ran to his car and took off before things settled down. So, that's where things are."

"I need to talk to you about your making-nice skills and about Doc, so I'll see you at the Bowlarama in an hour."

I arrived early and found the bowling alley mostly deserted. I tossed the case file on the table and sat down. Chester Atkins brought me a cup of coffee, grunted a "howdy," and departed. A few minutes later, the Reverend Billy Tripp ambled up to the table and lowered his massive posterior into the chair across from me. I will admit that the first thought that crossed my mind was how much weight the old wooden chair could hold.

"So how's my favorite atheist?" he asked.

Billy was not really an ordained preacher, but a paroled felon who, by accident or providence, had gotten on the wrong bus and ended up in Lyle. The townsfolk thought he was their replacement minister, and he played the part. That was sixteen years ago, and he's been playing the part ever since. When he's not fretting over his hook ball, he is a voracious reader. He might be as close to an intellectual as Lyle has to offer.

I offered him a coffee or beer but he waved it all off. "Just need to tie my shoe. Takes me a while to get my leg up so I can reach my foot." He tugged on his pants leg with both hands and forced his left leg across his right knee. "So I hear you've got yourself another murder investigation," he said affably. "Last killing prompted questions about chimpanzees, the treatment of animals, and the Great Chain of Being. I thoroughly enjoyed that exercise. Any moral underpinnings of this killing that we can chat about?"

My Aunt Sarah joined us. "I thought you were done with investigating murders. Now you got Doc in a state. Like old times." She turned to Billy. "What's up with you?"

"Shep was about to tell me if the murder he's investigating has an ethical component that is worthy of discussion," replied Billy.

"Eugenics," I said.

"Ah yes, the science that was supposed to provide a rational basis for racism. Being prejudiced is such a nasty state. But if it can be couched in scientific principles, we can be free of the moral burden that comes with hating someone who might be a different color or religion."

"I doubt most people have ever heard of it. I guess I shouldn't be surprised that you have."

Billy pursed his lips. "Well, you might be surprised to learn that, in prison, I was once a member of a skinhead group called the White Brothers."

"I'll go out on a limb and guess that that's not the name of a bowling team."

"Nope." Billy lowered his left leg, then repeated the shoelace tying process with the right leg. "We were dedicated to beating the crap out of non-whites. I never really understood why, but when you're young and in prison for the first time, feeling safe is more important than loving your fellow man. Predictably, there was a brawl. I watched as these men punched and bit each other for no discernible reason. Since I didn't join the fight, my membership in the White Brothers was short-lived. I got to know some of the older inmates, and one them told me about eugenics. I found some old books in the prison library and read them."

Chester came by the table, nodded at me, and said to Billy, "I've got you set up on lanes twelve and thirteen."

"It wasn't all about racism," said Sarah. "I mean do you really want a jailbird with six kids he can't support having more? That's someone that needs to be neutered like an old tom cat."

"I'm sure most people would agree with you," replied Billy, "but the argument is without merit. It always comes down to who decides and what the criteria are. Three crimes? Two kids? Four kids? I think history shows us that giving that power to the government produces lots of unintended consequences."

Sarah glowered at him, "Jesus, you don't have to get all preachy," she said standing. "I was just saying." She managed one more dismissive stare for each of us, then turned and walked away.

Billy dropped his right foot to the floor but didn't stand up. "To Sarah's point, not all eugenics was about race. But keeping the race pure for the good of the species seems to be one modern invention we could have lived without. I'd like to think we've come to our senses because we don't teach eugenics in school anymore. Of course, another reason for not teaching it is that it would make our elders look like racists. If you're interested, get a copy of *The Passing of the Great Race* published in 1916. It was a best seller, so it reflects the beliefs of its time. Some still believe it."

He stood and stamped his feet. "Without belaboring the point, a lot of what we find immoral in the Nazis' treatment of minorities was learned from America. We passed laws prohibiting blacks from marrying whites to keep the white race pure, and we enacted sterilization laws to keep undesirables from procreating. We wrote stringent immigration laws that limited the number of foreigners who could come to America. Asians were not allowed at all. We promoted the concept of a pure race—an Aryan race if you will."

"But didn't anyone see how crazy the notion of a pure race was?"

Billy laughed. "I'm sure some did, but they would have come up against folks like Theodore Roosevelt, Woodrow Wilson, Winston Churchill, Alexander Graham Bell, Margaret Sanger, and H. G. Wells. The eugenicists had money and prestige. Lots of work was performed at Harvard, Yale, Princeton, Stanford, and Johns Hopkins. Research was funded by the Carnegie and Rockefeller Foundations. The gene police thought they were doing God's work. Opposing voices were just drowned out."

"We never talk about it," I said.

"I would like to say that we've learned from our mistakes, but it's hard to be optimistic."

Billy headed to the lanes. A moment later, Robbie arrived. "We're going to get something straight here and now. You won't be cutting me out of this investigation. Everything you learn, you will tell me about without me having to browbeat you. Any place you go, I'm going. Tell me that's understood and agreed to, and I'll tell you something you don't know."

"Message received and agreed."

"The good news is that Doc Adams heard back from Ruth Littleton's sister. Her caretaker is still alive. That's what he told Sarah anyway. The bad news is that Doc isn't inclined to tell you who she is and where she lives. Apparently, when he called the caretaker, she got real upset. Doc's back to not wanting to dredge up the past, and his mind is made up."

I placed a plastic bag of small bones on the table. "These are some of the bones that Gaylord found on the hospital grounds. They could be animal bones, but to me they look like little fingers. If I'm right, dredging up the past is exactly what we should be doing."

"You know Doc. He's not going to just change his mind because of some bones."

I patted the case file. "How badly do you want to know why someone killed Abigail Nichols and what happened to the baby?"

Robbie glanced at the file folder and the bones and gave me an uncertain look. "Why are you asking me that?"

"Because there are gruesome photos in this folder of what Abigail looked like after being beaten."

"And you want to show them to Doc?" she asked incredulously.

"Getting information from people is not always a pleasant task," I said. "We have to decide how important the information is and what we are willing to do to get it. I know Doc's an old man, but right now he's the only lead we have. Reggie's on the verge of spilling his guts to a prosecutor. And I need to know what went on at Sweetwater. If we need answers, we can't be worrying about being nice."

Robbie stared at the folder. "Show me."

I opened the file. "Are you sure you want to see this?"

When she nodded, I slid the crime scene photo of Abigail Nichols as she was found by the police. Robbie recoiled, then jumped from her chair. "For the love of God, how could someone do that to an old woman? Jesus!"

"Doc has to know that the person who did this to Abigail may still be out there and needs to be found. He also needs to know what happened to children at the Sweetwater Hospital when no one was looking."

Doc's house and office was a fifteen-minute walk from the bowling alley. He lived and worked on a residential street lined with old houses and older trees. The sun was bright, and the air, despite the remaining snow pack, was warm and sweet smelling. Birds were busily feasting on newly filled feeders. The voices of children playing could be heard even if they remained unseen.

We climbed the stairs to a covered porch that wrapped around Doc's frame house. The door opened before we could knock. "What part of 'I don't want to talk about it' did you not understand?" he asked, joining us.

"The part of me that doesn't let blind stubbornness stand in the way of doing the right thing," I replied.

"You sound more like your mother all the time," he replied, "and that ain't no compliment."

As he turned to go inside, I handed him the photograph and the bag of bones.

"The bones are the remains of babies killed by the doctors at Sweetwater Hospital," I said. "The picture shows what happened to Abigail. You look at these and see if you change your mind. We'll wait out here."

"Then you'll be here all night."

The door slammed, leaving Robbie staring at me. "You were a little harsh," she said.

"I was exercising restraint," I said.

Robbie sat on a bench. "So what did Agent Bauer want exactly?"

"He's trying to figure out whether to trust me or not. I think he wanted to see if I had spent my inheritance on expensive art and cars instead of dealing with Reilly's taxes. Seeing the way I live was probably helpful. But after my tiff with Reggie, I'm not sure what he thinks."

"I don't understand the way you live, so I doubt he could."

To my relief, Robbie didn't pursue the issue further.

"I saw Gloria Strap the other day," I said casually. "She seems to be getting worse."

"Her sister Roslyn is worried about her," said Robbie, "but they don't have enough money to pay anyone to take care of her. Roslyn tries to keep an eye on her, but it isn't easy. Gloria refuses to move to town. It's tough"

"What do you think will happen to her farm when she's institutional-ized?"

Robbie studied me for moment. "Why would you care?"

The truthful answer was that my vision for version two of the poor farm required acquisition of her farm. But I wasn't yet ready to have that conversation with Robbie and sought refuge in a plausible response. "I like the neighborhood the way it is," I said. "I wouldn't want some noisy neighbors moving in and ruining things."

"Talk to Roslyn. Her number's in the card file on my desk." A few more minutes passed.

"You don't have to stay," I said.

"Yes I do."

I paced across the porch until Robbie insisted that I either sit down or leave. I was about to sit when the front door opened and Doc shuffled out on the porch. He handed the photograph, the bones, and a piece of paper to me. "Sorry if I touched a nerve," I said.

"Son, you don't touch nerves. You hit them with both hands. All of this rummaging through the past does no good. But whoever did this... killing babies..." Doc groaned softly. "The caretaker you want to talk to is Carla Davis. She's being taken care of by Margo Strauss, her niece. She lives in Manassas, not too far from here. Margo wasn't too keen on you visiting her and bringing up the past and all because it upsets Carla, but I told her you just had a few questions and were trying to solve a murder. Margo wanted to know if she'd be on TV. I told her she might, so there's that. Anyway, she's expecting you tomorrow morning."

"Thanks, Doc," said Robbie.

"Whoever butchered that woman won't hesitate to kill you both. Don't you two do anything stupid. I don't want to regret helping you." He sighed and went inside.

Robbie looked at me. "Probably too late to consider not being stupid"

"Pretty much."

CHAPTER 12
Saturday, February 16

I spent the first part of the evening at home looking over a plat of the poor farm and imagining where I would build housing and other facilities for the new residents. I pursued this exercise until it became clear that I had no idea what I was doing.

Reluctantly, I turned my attention to the file of Abigail's murder. Reggie had acquired lots of photos and hand-drawn diagrams of the crime scene. There also were interviews with neighbors. Most of the interviews were of the short "I didn't see nothing unusual" variety. One neighbor reported seeing a truck and a man running from the garage. Albert Loftus was picked up a few hours after the murder based on an anonymous tip and instantly became the prime suspect. Because the evidence against Albert was so compelling, further analysis of the crime scene evidence was suspended. As with my attempt to design a new poor farm, my attempt to glean information from a crime report was hampered by a lack of skill and training. Even so, I stared at the photos and drawings, confident that determination could overcome ignorance. But if the file had a story to tell, I couldn't hear it.

Around ten, I gave up and crawled into bed. My feline companions took their spots on the bedspread. With the lights out, I closed my eyes to a chorus of bathing and purring. I was on the serene edge of sleep when I was pulled back by an image of Abigail's kitchen. I rolled out of bed, retrieved the crime scene folder, and looked again at the pictures of Abigail's house. Except for the white ceramic cup that contained Willet's DNA, the kitchen was clean and orderly. The towels were hung straight from bars attached to the cabinets. The sink was empty. The dishes, including the cup used by Baby John, had been placed in the dishwasher. I resisted drawing any conclusions about Willet and his sister's murder.

But I was suddenly flush with questions about when he was at the house and why he was there.

———————————

I picked Robbie up at around nine and headed toward Manassas. Robbie was chatty and in good spirits.

"I had breakfast with the Residents this morning. Carrie told me that when Abigail came to the farm, the farm supported more than twenty tenants, many of them veterans who couldn't find work or who had trouble reentering civilian life. It was still an active farm. Harry and Cecil spent the day working the fields and Carrie helped in the kitchen and the garden. They didn't see much of Abigail, and she did her best to avoid them. Carrie said that one day, she saw Abigail coming from the basement. Carrie remembered that Abigail had coal dust on her hands. What was she doing in the basement of your house?"

We spent a few minutes speculating about what might have taken Abigail into the depths of the poor farm's basement, and settled on the idea that she was hiding from someone, then slipped into a comfortable silence.

We took the John Marshall Highway to I-66. The rolling hills were covered by patches of snow that glistened in the bright morning sun. A colt ran and darted toward its indifferent mother. On the southern slopes where the snow had fully melted, the pale green hues of new grass hinted at the approaching spring. Life was in the process of renewing itself, even as we were mired in the story of a life that had ended too soon.

We found Margo Strauss' house in an older suburb of Manassas. Time and a lack of money had taken its toll on the neighborhood, but Margo's home was the exception. Brightly painted in Florida colors of pale blues, yellows, and coral, I would not have been surprised to find Jimmy Buffet in residence singing Margaritaville. While the house was welcoming, Margo was not.

"I don't know what you expect to accomplish by badgering an old frail woman," she said as we stepped inside. "Doc Adams is a son-of-a-bitch sometimes and wouldn't take no for an answer. Something about a doctor killing babies. Carla doesn't know anything about that and, if she did, she couldn't tell you without going all to pieces. All you're going to do is upset her and leave me with trying to fix it."

"I'm Shep and this is Robbie," I said after Margo was finished.

Robbie offered her hand but Margo turned away. "She's in there watching TV. Do what you have to do and leave."

We followed Margo's gaze to a small room where a white-haired woman sat in a recliner. Carla was petite and looked almost doll-like in the large chair. She glanced at us, but her attention was on a Tom and Jerry cartoon.

"The mouse always wins," she said. "I'd like to see Tom win once"

"Cheering for the undercat," I said.

The remark, which I thought was funny, had no effect on Carla.

Robbie and I took seats on either side of Carla and watched as Jerry put a firecracker under Tom's tail. Carla looked at her watch and changed the channel to MSNBC.

"The market just opened," she said. "I bought Apple stock last week at 13. Mark my words, sometime down the road, thirteen bucks is gonna look mighty good. I may not make it down the road that far, but you will, so go all in." Carla let out a laugh that defied her diminutive size. "The long run may just be too long for me. That's a fact. But I like thinking positive, you know."

"Would you mind if we asked you about your time at Lady of Comfort?" I asked.

With her eyes glued to the screen, Carla shrugged and said, "Why would I mind, honey?"

"Margo said that it upsets you to talk about the past," said Robbie. "We're not here to upset you."

Carla clicked off the TV. "For the love of God, I wish she'd stop telling people that crap about me. Margo is a manic depressive. She's on every medication you can take and drinks too much. She tells everyone she's taking care of me, but I moved in here to make sure she didn't finally succeed in killing herself. Frankly, it would be a relief if she did, but that's not terribly empathetic, so I try to keep those thoughts to myself. Anyway, get to your point so I can do some trading." She laughed again. "Sorry for yelling, sweetie. Just get a little riled up sometimes. No offense intended."

"No offense taken," replied Robbie.

"You may have heard about a woman named Jennifer Rice being murdered in her home near Winchester," I said.

"Right," replied Carla, focusing her gaze on me for the first time. "Oh my God. You're Mary's son! I knew your real papa, Reilly Heartwood. You turned out good for a fella who went to prison."

"Jennifer Rice was actually Abigail Nichols," I said.

"What about Abigail?"

It took a moment for the realities to sink in. "Well, that just don't seem right! Abigail murdered. Who would think she'd die like that? She was so good to Ruth. Murdered? This world has gone to shit."

I suppressed a smile.

"We know that Abigail took a black baby boy and that Ruth helped her. We're trying to find the child and reunite him with his birth mother. We were hoping you might know where Abigail went, what she named him—anything to help us find him."

"That was a long time ago," said Carla.

"If you could just try," said Robbie encouragingly.

"I didn't say I didn't remember. I just said it was a long time ago. For Christ's sake, I'm old but not brain dead."

I barely contained a laugh, relieved that I hadn't fallen into the trap that had snagged Robbie.

"Ruth was a high energy, nervous woman," continued Carla. "According to her husband, she'd experience episodes in which she would suddenly wake up frightened and disoriented. These mini-breakdowns lasted a few days or so, after which she'd get better. She wouldn't remember much about what happened, just that she was overwhelmed with thoughts and images and sounds, like what they called a bad trip in the sixties. She was aware that she was out of control but helpless to orient herself. When Abigail showed up with the baby, Ruth was excited. But when Abigail explained what her father was doing, Ruth started to slip.

She managed for a while, but her tether to reality broke for good and she came to Lady of Comfort. I was the only one who could calm her, bathe her, or feed her."

"Did you ever meet Abigail?" I asked.

"Not in person, but I got to know her through the letters she wrote to Ruth. Lots of times the letters bore postmarks from an exotic location. When they arrived, I believe I was more excited than Ruth. I used to read them to her and, for a time, it seemed as if she was actually trying to follow what Abigail was saying."

"Did Abigail mention the child?" I asked.

"Paul was his first name," replied Carla. "Give me a second…Thomas. Yup. Paul Thomas. He traveled with her when he wasn't in school."

"Can you think of any reason anyone would want to kill Abigail?" asked Robbie.

Carla shook her head. "No. She never wrote anything that made me think she was in trouble. Of course, the letters stopped when Ruth died forty years ago." Carla must have read the disappointment in my face. "I have the letters in a box if you'd like to read them."

I said I did and she disappeared from the room.

"Feisty lady," I said. "I might buy some of that stock she mentioned"

"Let's hope there's something more to go on in those letters."

We took the letters and thanked Carla for her help. The last thing she said was something about buying stock in an Internet company called Google when it went public. Robbie laughed at the name and wondered how long it would last.

When I reached the car, I called Gus and asked him to conduct a search for Paul Thomas. We agreed to limit the search to Virginia and the states that bordered it. When he asked if that was all, I tossed out the names of Albert Loftus and Kyle Hopper.

"What was that about?" asked Robbie, "I understand asking about Albert, Paul, and the hospital, but what's with the question about Kyle? He was pretty helpful the other day and seemed to care for some of the older residents of Sweetwater. I thought we decided he wasn't a serial killer"

"Right now I'm not sure who's a good guy and who isn't. Kyle may not be a serial killer, but he's a player in this little drama, and it pays to know who you're dealing with."

As we headed back to the interstate, I told Robbie about the photograph of Abigail's kitchen showing the cup that Willet had used. She removed the picture from the case file and studied it for a few minutes. "I understand that the cup seems out of place, but I don't see that it means anything."

"I don't see it," I said, "but I feel it. I think Willet was there the day his sister was killed."

"You think he killed her?"

"Sort of, but objectively I have no proof that he did or didn't."

"Back to something tangible. Let's say we find Paul and decide that he's the killer. We just can't walk up to him, introduce ourselves, and ask him to talk about his mother."

"Actually, that is—or was—the plan. If we don't threaten him, we should be okay."

"I can see you've thought this through," said Robbie. "Basically, if we treat the killer nicely, he will be nice to us."

"The plan's a work in progress. Let's not nit-pick."

Robbie returned her attention to the case file. I turned on the radio and found a light jazz station. Believing that the conversation had ended, I turned the volume up on the radio, but Robbie reached over and turned the radio off. "Why did you ask me about buying Gloria Strap's farm?"

The question caught me off guard. "I told you. I just wanted to be certain who my neighbors are if Gloria has to sell."

"But you can't be thinking of staying on the farm much longer?"

My silence was met with a cold stare. "I know you thought about this." She studied me for a moment. "Oh my God! You have thought about it! You have a plan. I don't understand why you won't talk to me about it."

"You know better than I that Reilly had a plan for the farm. His plan failed and people lost money"

"Which means what?"

I went through the scenario I had described to Reggie. Robbie stared at me, stunned into silence.

"Okay," I said after a moment. "That sounds like so much do-gooder happy talk. So let's drop it."

Robbie's face brightened. "Oh my God," she said laughing. "That's such an awesome idea I can't get my head wrapped around it. I think you're nuts. So how do you open a poor farm exactly?"

"Not a clue."

The conversation that ensued was animated, creative, and replete with optimism. As I turned onto the interstate, we were throwing out ideas for providing training to adults, education to children, and a place for animals that had been abandoned or mistreated. We were still lost in our idealistic world when the phone rang.

"I think we found your Paul Thomas," said Gus, "which is the good news. I've got some serious questions about the owners of the Sweetwater Hospital."

"How serious?" I asked.

"I'm getting a chopper," said Gus. "I'll meet you at the farm."

CHAPTER 13
Saturday February 16

I saw Gus on the porch of the main house. He was leaning against a post and smoking a pipe. He smoked his pipe infrequently, but on reflection, it was usually a precursor to bad news. Robbie spent the last hour of the drive from Manassas speculating on what could be so important that Gus would fly out to explain it to us. After an hour of what ifs, I was eager to get to the facts, no matter what.

I gave Gus the now well-practiced explanation as to why we couldn't go into the main house and led him to the bunkhouse. We sat at the kitchen table. In response to an offer of something to drink or eat, Gus simply replied, "Let's get to it."

From his briefcase he removed a stack of files, selected one, and handed it to me. "I learned this morning that the FBI was keeping a file on Abigail Nichols. Apparently, she was writing letters to prominent people, asking them to publicly apologize for their family's involvement in research that used minorities as test subjects and for their support of medical experiments performed on Jews during the war. This letter was received five years ago by an FBI field director whose father held anti-Semitic views. Look at the last sentence."

I read the sentence out loud. "If you do not comply with this letter, I will release records to the major media outlets that will disclose extensive details of your family's involvement in these activities and more."

"The second page has a long list of people supposedly copied on the letter, but when the FBI checked with them, they all denied receiving it.

In just a second, I'll get to the names that are highlighted. So you know, the remaining documents in the file are reports of field agents explaining that they could not find any information about the whereabouts of Abigail Nichols. I included them so you wouldn't ask, but there's really no point wasting your time looking for them."

"Emma said that Abigail had some of her father's papers that would protect Paul. If someone believed that she would actually release them," said Robbie, "that would be a motive for murder."

Gus removed a stack of papers from his briefcase and unfolded them to display a chart arranged with the Anderson Historical Foundation at the top and rows of multiple boxes below. Eight boxes were highlighted in yellow.

"The foundation is structured just like a typical corporation. Basically, it's not a charity. The foundation purchased the Sweetwater Hospital and some of the other buildings in town. The stockholders include individuals, partnerships, and other corporate entities. I'm still not sure we know all of the individuals involved, but at this point, it doesn't actually matter. Now look at the names highlighted in yellow on the chart and the highlighted names on the blackmail letter. It appears that the recipients of the letter organized to acquire the hospital, the old Nichols house, and a few other properties. You should note that some of the recipients of the letter are congressmen, judges, and CEOs. This is what you're up against."

"Did any of the recipients comply with her demands?" I asked.

"No. A few months later, a second letter went out demanding money and threatening disclosure of even more damaging information. We don't know if anyone paid, but no one offered a public apology for the alleged activities."

I studied the chart for a moment. "I seriously doubt that Abigail wrote the letters. She didn't need the money. It's odd that no one took the threat seriously enough to apologize but were so concerned that they bought a house and a hospital in the middle of nowhere."

"Why would these people buy an old hospital and house?" asked Robbie. "I don't get it."

"Who knows how rich people think," said Gus. When I laughed, he added, "You were an enigma before you got rich. One possible inference is that they believed that more documents like the ones mentioned in her letter were hidden at the hospital and in the house. That's just a guess."

Robbie grimaced. "So now we have at least eight additional suspects we can identify, any of whom may have wanted Abigail dead."

Gus gathered the papers from the table. "Eight that are named. The other stockholders are corporate entities that could be shielding someone with something to hide. If Jennifer Rice was killed by one of the foundation owners, then someone figured out that she was actually Abigail Nichols. With your visit to Sweetwater, and your conversation with Kyle Hopper, it isn't a big leap that you also know who Jennifer really was. Following this line of thought to its logical conclusion, the foundation owners may now view you as a threat, which of course is the very situation you said you would avoid."

I ignored Gus' rebuke. "What did you find about Kyle Hopper?"

Gus opened another file. "He was a detective in New Jersey. He wasn't promoted despite good test scores. He had a reputation with his peers of not being a team player. His partner was investigated for shooting an unarmed suspect. At a grand jury hearing, he refused to back up his partner's claim that the suspect had drawn a gun. He testified instead that he hadn't seen the actual shooting—testimony that pissed off his partner, other cops, and the prosecutor.

"Later, he was accused by a Federal task force of being corrupt, which seems like payback for not backing up his partner. On top of that, his partner was his wife's brother-in-law. His wife divorced Kyle, alleging spousal abuse. He took to drinking and gambling. His gambling debts disappeared after a witness was shot dead before testifying in front of a grand jury investigating the guy he owed money to. Kyle was never indicted and took disability retirement. It's hard to say what he might do, but I wouldn't put a lot of faith in what he tells you."

"It's a little late for that, but thanks. So what about Paul Thomas?"

"We have several candidates for your guy, but the one who stands out is a sociology professor at Jefferson College. He's the right age, color, and mindset."

"I know you're good and all, but how can you tell about his mindset?" asked Robbie.

"The gentleman described in this biography is rather famous within sociology circles for his writings about eugenics," he replied. "He also published a book of poems. I must admit that I had to look up eugenics and that I don't know much about poetry. But he doesn't seem to be a happy man. Read this and tell me what you think."

He handed each of us a page containing a poem entitled Faded Genes.

Am I white?
Am I black?
Am I what I seem? Oh, to be cursed By faded genes.
My blood is impure
I can't marry a white,
But I'm not a black man My skin is too light.
I am a stranger to both races, I'm caught in between
A victim for life
Of my faded genes.

Robbie tossed the paper on to the table and leaned back in her chair. "This just gets more and more painful to deal with," she said. "The guy's kidnapped so he won't be killed by a doctor working with Abigail's father. He grows up not knowing who the hell he is, and Abigail is murdered by some rich guys who are hiding something."

"Listen to me, both of you. You don't know who killed Abigail or why. It could have to do with the foundation or it may have been about something else entirely. Her brother or Paul may have had a reason to kill her. Even Albert Loftus may have killed her. Given the complexity of the case and the inability to definitively identify who killed Abigail, you need to accept that it's too dangerous for you to be playing detective."

"We can't tell the cops what we know because of Reggie," I said. "He's our client. He asked us to find his cousin so we can reunite his aunt with her son. That's what we're going to do."

"You're making a mistake, but I know better than to argue with you." He handed me another file folder. "This is information about Albert Loftus. He doesn't look like a killer, but he's had some bad luck. He got a job and managed to stay out of trouble for a while. Then he hurt his leg in an accident and was let go. I could see how that might make him angry enough to revert to his old ways. Beating an old woman to death seems a bit extreme, but the capacity of humans to cause misery to others has ceased to surprise me."

"How bad was his leg injury?" I asked.

"Torn knee ligaments. If I remember correctly, he wears a brace and walks with a noticeable limp. Is that important?"

I looked at Robbie. "Yeah. I think it is. Thanks."

Gus again declined refreshments and boarded the helicopter. The cats scrambled under the bed as the copter lifted off. Robbie followed me to the living room.

"Okay. So what are you not telling me now?"

I reached for the case file that Reggie left and handed her the transcript of the anonymous caller. "The tipster said that he saw a man running out of the front of the house."

Robbie looked at the transcript. "So?"

"Albert can't run. He wears a brace and walks with a limp. That means that Albert was set up. Someone put the jewelry in his car, watched him leave, and called the police." I handed her another document. "A neighbor reported seeing a man running from the garage. The police assumed that it was two people seeing the same thing, albeit from different angles. I think the neighbor saw the real killer, and it wasn't Albert. The tip to police came from the killer."

"I assume the prosecution is aware of the case's weakness," said Robbie. "Certainly the defense counsel will figure this out. This could be good news."

I shook my head. "Under these circumstances, Albert will be offered a plea bargain to avoid the death penalty. Basically, go to trial and risk death or agree to a life sentence. Given that Albert has no money, his attorney isn't going to want to put up much of a fight. Life in prison is still a death sentence, only a slow and cruel one for an innocent man. Of course, if we tell Reggie that Albert's innocent, he will disclose what he knows to the prosecutor."

"So what do we do?"

"Because of our representation of Reggie, we can't intercede on Albert's behalf. Albert's and Reggie's fates are in our hands, and for now they seem to be tied together."

"Unless we find out who actually killed Abigail"

"That's seems to be where we are."

Robbie handed the reports back to me. "Maybe it's time to let Reggie talk to Detective Hunter and explain what we've learned. That would clear Albert, and I think Reggie would feel better."

I slipped the reports into the file and tossed it onto the café table. "I'm sure the prosecutor would be really pleased with Reggie coming forward and exonerating Albert. No jail time in exchange for blowing up the prosecution's case."

"If you're going to get snarky, then I'm free to remind you that you said learning the truth leads to hard choices. You don't want Reggie going to jail. Great. But you know that the odds of you finding out who killed Abigail are pretty slim. Tell Reggie and let him make the choice. I know it sucks, but that's where we are."

Robbie was right, but I fought against admitting it. "How about we talk to Paul tomorrow? Maybe we can eliminate him from the suspect list. Then I can call Reggie and tell him what we know."

"I don't see how that will change anything, but I want to hear what Paul has to say. I mean, the story is as fascinating as it is tragic."

"I need to talk to the Residents about the letters Abigail wrote to Ruth, so I can drop you off in town. I'll pick you up in the morning about eight thirty, and we'll see what Paul has to tell us."

———————————

When I arrived at Heartwood House, the Residents were in full rebellion. The wireless network had gone down and Cecil, Harry, and Carrie were busy blaming each other while trying to restart it. Apparently, Harry had read something on the web about adding a security key and now no one could log on. Cecil decided he could fix the network by resetting the router to its factory default settings, but that changed the network name, the encryption key, and the administrative login name and password. Lora Jean joined the fray when she lost connection to a chat room and demanded that someone fix the network immediately.

All of this became my problem the moment I stepped into Heartwood House. I connected a laptop to the router and logged into the router interface using a browser. I was in the process of restoring the settings when more bickering broke out about who told whom to do the things I was doing. Finally, I shooed them all from the study and shut the door, but even then I could hear accusations and denials, mostly about how angry I was and whose fault it was. These were the symptoms of cabin fever.

With the household reconnected to the Internet, I opened the door to the study and found three worried faces staring at me. "I need help with my murder case, but you have to promise me you can get along."

"We weren't angry at each other," said Carrie.

"I wasn't," said Harry.

"Me neither," agreed Cecil.

"I think Shep just misunderstood because he has tax problems," said Carrie.

I didn't even try to follow the logic of that statement. "That's probably what happened."

Back in the study, I put the letters on the desk. "The blonde woman with the baby was named Abigail Nichols. Sadly, she was also known by the name Jennifer Rice."

"That means she's dead?" asked Harry.

"I'm afraid she is."

Harry lowered his head and took a slow, deep breath. Carrie patted his hand.

"Before Abigail was murdered, she wrote letters to Ruth Littleton. I need you to read the letters and see if Abigail said anything that would help us find out who killed her."

Carrie took the bundle of letters from the table and held them reverently in both hands. "These are private letters," she said. "I don't think it's right to read them."

"But we want to find out who killed her," said Harry.

"How about we do this?" I said. "You all read the letters. You decide what's personal and what isn't. Personal matters you keep secret, even from me. Then you can sign a promise not to tell anyone else about the secret parts."

"That works," said Carrie.

"I'll get yellow pads," said Cecil.

"If you find anything important, you call me."

I went through the kitchen to the sunroom on the south side of the house. This had always been my favorite place to sit, especially on a cold sunny day. Reilly would sometimes join me with his guitar and strum chords. Today, the sunroom was occupied by a pair of cats, each of whom took turns glaring at me for disturbing the tranquility.

I sat in a cushioned chair washed in a sunbeam and closed my eyes. I was eager to enjoy the moment and to stop the chatter in my head, but the effort was futile. My future and Abigail's past took turns spewing out questions I couldn't answer.

I opened my eyes to find Frieda carrying two cups of some steaming beverage. To my surprise and delight, it was cider with a stick of cinnamon and a splash of rum. "You look like you've got the weight of the world on your shoulders, Shep. This might help lighten the load."

She gently lifted a small cat from the chair next to me, sat down, and put the cat in her lap. The feline spun around twice, then flopped over and purred loudly.

"I think I owe you an apology," she said, rubbing the cat under the chin.

"Me or the feline?"

"You of course. I complain a lot about you getting involved in things. I don't want you to get hurt. I couldn't abide you getting yourself killed. But I haven't said how proud I am that you want to make things right. Reilly had that quality. I think he'd be proud of you, too."

"That's nice to hear," I said.

We drank cider as the sun sank toward the horizon and for a short while, my head was noiseless and thought-free.

CHAPTER 14
Sunday, February 17

I spent the early morning inspecting the main house, even venturing inside for a few minutes. The house was dying a slow death. New cracks had appeared in the ceiling and the walls along the back of the structure. The floor in the kitchen was sagging noticeably. As Markus instructed, I went into the basement and tightened the support post. When I heard a loud snap from the timber above the post, I bolted up the steps.

I stood in the foyer with the front door open for a few minutes and allowed fresh memories to wash over me. My mother was there, Reilly Heartwood was there, and Doc stood there. I could hear voices and smell the rich aromas of fried chicken and okra. The images were so real that I thought I could touch them, embrace them, and taste them. I was engulfed by an immense sadness of what was no more, and ran outside before the weight of the moment was too great to bear.

Robbie called and asked that I meet her at Heartwood House. When I arrived, I followed loud voices to the kitchen where Frieda, the four Residents, Lora Jean, and Robbie were engaged in an animated conversation. I heard Harry in mid-sentence say, "and then Shep thought the snake was a stick and…" followed by peals of laughter. When my presence was noted, the laughter paused briefly before erupting again.

"Don't mind me," I said, feigning indignation. "Please feel free to laugh at the traumatic experiences suffered by an innocent child."

Cecil took me literally. "That had to be one of funniest damn things I ever seen. When that stick moved, old Shep tried to run so fast he ran into the fence. Yeah, that was good for a chuckle for years."

"Perhaps on our drive today, you and I should talk about your feelings toward the live stick," said Robbie in a patronizing tone.

"Perhaps we won't talk at all," I replied.

After laughter died down, I asked Lora Jean for her phone. The request seemed to concern her, and the fact that she was concerned made Frieda concerned. After assuring Lora Jean that I only wanted to make a phone call to be certain Paul was at home, and that I wasn't going to look at any of the pictures, emails, or texts on her phone, we agreed that she could dial the number and ask for Charlie. Carrie wanted to know who Charlie was and more conversation ensued. Robbie couldn't contain her laughter at how a simple request had become such a complex negotiation.

Laura Jean made the call. "I'm sorry," she said. "I must have called the wrong number." At that, I stood up and headed to the car.

The weather had turned cold again. A few crocuses that had proudly emerged from the ground during the brief thaw paid the price for impatience. Hopefully, the others would wait until it was safer.

Robbie insisted on driving and using her GPS device to navigate. After hearing "recalculating" a dozen times, I shut it off and retrieved a map from my backpack. Once on route 29 South, there wasn't much navigating to do.

For the next thirty minutes, I played with Robbie's GPS unit. I managed to reprogram Paul's address and confirmed that the instructions matched the route suggested by the map. We turned west a few miles outside of Charlottesville and wove our way through a web of back roads until the GPS announced that we should turn left. Robbie slowed, but still almost missed the entrance to Paul's house.

Unlike the driveway to the poor farm, this road was paved and well maintained. The pavement ended in a circular driveway formed from cobblestones. Even in the dead of winter, a fountain in the middle of the circle was flowing. At the base of the fountain, small wisps of steam rose from the pool before being whisked away by the wind.

Paul's house was made of gray stone set off by large glass windows. The house was on a knoll overlooking a partially frozen lake. A flock of ducks huddled on the ice, probably wishing they had gone south with their friends. We rang the doorbell and waited. I heard a whirring sound and looked up to see a camera zooming in for a closer look. A moment later, we were greeted by a voice from an intercom system.

"Say your names and what you want."

We identified ourselves. "We are here to talk to you about Jennifer Rice," I said.

The intercom was briefly silent before it crackled to life.

"Take the sidewalk to the right and you'll see the greenhouse. Close the first door before you open the second. Some of my plants are cold sensitive."

"That was creepy," said Robbie as we made our way to the back of the house. "Might you have brought your gun, you know, just in case Paul has something to hide?"

"Sorry, no gun. But if you like, I can look for a really big stick that looks like a snake."

We arrived at the greenhouse and entered through the outer door. As instructed, we waited until it closed. The small ante room was comfortable but not warm. When Robbie opened the inner door, we were met by a blast of hot and humid air that carried an earthy aroma of wet humus mixed with an unfamiliar sweet scent that instantly made me think of spring. We unbuttoned our jackets and quickly removed them. We followed the sound of someone humming, then passed through a stand of banana trees in large pots on our way to its source.

Paul was a tall, lean man dressed in shorts and a faded black t-shirt. I could still see the words, "I can't tolerate intolerant people" emblazoned on the back in cracked red ink. His hair was pulled back into a pony tail. A graying stubble grew in clumps on his cheeks and neck, but not much was visible on his chin. His hands were covered with black earth. He didn't look at us as we approached, but his body language was friendly.

"I still get a thrill picking a banana grown in the middle of winter in Virginia," he said. "Of course, the ones I grow cost me about ten dollars a pound."

When he looked up, I was struck by his dark eyes. He smiled but continued working on a clump of roots.

"I feel compelled to explain to my green friends that my house and greenhouse are warmed by solar water heaters, solar voltaic panels, and a geothermal system that cuts my carbon footprint to less than the average homeless person." He laughed again. "Always defensive. Even to people who don't ask."

Paul picked up a small machete and gave us a cold look. Robbie stepped back. Although denying it, I had slipped a small automatic into the pocket of my coat. I had my hand on the grip from the moment we stepped into the greenhouse. With a quick chop, Paul split the clump of roots into two pieces. He inspected them, split each of them again, and tossed the machete onto a small table.

Paul nodded. "How did you find me?"

"Your DNA was found in Jennifer Rice's home where she was found murdered a few weeks ago," I said, my response intentionally vague.

"My DNA led you here? And you're not cops?"

"No," said Robbie. "We're attorneys."

"Funny how that sounds only incrementally less threatening," said Paul. "Well, okay then. I must say that I'm surprised by your visit and a little miffed at the invasion of my privacy, a state that has apparently deprived me of my manners. I propose that we sit and get to know each other better."

"Before we become friends," I said, "I need to ask if you killed Jennifer Rice, and if you didn't, if you know who did?"

"Mr. Harrington, your legal training presses you to come right to the point," replied Paul. "I must say that it's refreshing to have guests whose agenda isn't hidden. I believe all of your questions are best answered while basking in the glorious sunshine of my patio."

He dunked his hands in a barrel of water, then rinsed again in a small sink. "I reclaim the water from my pond. It's very cold this time of year, but, after it runs through a half a mile of black pipe along the paved portion of my driveway, it rarely requires any further heating. This way."

He led us through rows of ripening tomatoes. We arrived at another air lock and entered a glass-enclosed patio overlooking the lake. The patio floor and back wall were black. A fan hummed softly. "The wall and floor are components of a passive solar heating system," Paul said, anticipating my question. He disappeared, leaving the two of us to contemplate the view.

"He's still a suspect," I said. "Even if he is quirky in a likeable way." Paul returned with a tray of cups and cakes and motioned for us to sit.

"I hope cappuccino suits everyone."

After we were all situated, Paul said, "To answer your questions, I didn't kill Jen. On the day she was murdered, I was here alone, which is not helpful, but believe me when I say, in a heartbeat I would kill whoever did it. I hear they have a suspect."

"They do, but we're not convinced he murdered Jennifer."

Paul nodded. "I'm sure it's disturbing for you to contemplate an innocent man going to prison."

Robbie started to speak but Paul cut her off with his hand. "Not yet, please. We are starting the narrative at the end of the story. Stories need to be told from beginning to end, although this one is incomplete."

A flock of ducks flew over the house and raised their wings in preparation for landing. "The lake is fed by warm waste water," said Paul. "Some of the ducks have developed a bad habit of staying the winter. Relying on others to keep you warm will get you killed." He shook his head. "Sorry. I'm prone to digressions, a consequence of living in isolation much of the time."

"The beginning," I said, coaxing him to return to the subject at hand.

"Right. To understand Jen, it is necessary to accept that you won't. She was a woman of vexing secrets whose past was shrouded in a fog of her own making. I never totally understood who she was, and for a child seeking an explanation for his own circumstances, this was more than a bit troubling. What I can say is that Jen was an opened-minded, generous person who saw a child in trouble and did something about it. Without boring you with the details, I was stolen from a hospital to save me from being euthanized because of the color of my skin. Before Jen took me in, I was apparently handed off a few times. She hired a black woman as a house keeper whose real job was to pretend to be my mother. This arrangement allowed Jen to live in Winchester without having to answer questions about being an unwed woman with a near-white baby." Paul shrugged. "I suppose it just added to my confusion, but that's what happened."

"She didn't live here?" asked Robbie.

"Jen had this built as a retreat. She found this spot as a child when attending a summer camp nearby. She used the royalties from her first book to buy the land and to build a small house, then added to it. I was in college when I learned that the property was put in my name. Again, she would never say why it was that way, but this place will always be more hers than mine."

"When did you learn the truth about who you were?" I asked.

"Taking 'truth' in the larger sense of the word, I was about eight when Jen explained that the housekeeper was not my mother. I had that figured out, but it was nice to hear it from Jen. About the same time, I also learned what it was to be 'not white.' I had been home-schooled for my first two years so I could travel with Jen. When the housekeeper left, Jen tried to put me in school with our white neighbors. At school I was called a nigger by some of the older kids, even though in the winter I looked almost as white as them. I held my own in the fights that ensued. Jen thought that it would all blow over, but then the school board informed her that I was not eligible to attend the all-white school." Paul laughed. "Why are liberals so naïve?"

"Did you attend the black school?" asked Robbie.

Paul laughed. "For a day. I wasn't wanted there either. I could pass for white, and many of the kids had reason to resent my presence. No. I was a kid who didn't belong anywhere."

Paul seemed to lose himself in the memory. He sighed several times before speaking again. "The next year, the schools were closed as part of the state's massive resistance to the federal order to integrate. Private schools opened, some in the public school buildings. If you were white and had enough money, you could pay to be educated. But there were no good alternatives for black kids or poor whites. Their educations were permanently stunted. I went back to being home-schooled until Jen moved us to DC, where the schools had been desegregated. I learned a lot about prejudice at a young age, including the privileges that came from being white"

"What privileges?" asked Robbie.

"The privilege of not being harassed when you walk into a rich neighborhood, of not being pulled over for minor traffic infractions, of being able to sit in a restaurant, go to a university, use a bathroom, drink from a water fountain, things like that. These are privileges that white people have solely because of their skin color. Whites have no idea about these privileges. Non-whites are well aware of them and fight for them. Sometimes, I could get away with using the white facilities, but sometimes I caught holy hell. That, I guess, is what an education is about. Another cappuccino?"

When neither of us protested, Paul took the tray and went inside.

I turned to Robbie. "He hasn't used the name Abigail," I whispered. "And he seems to believe that Jennifer Rice had nothing to do with his kidnapping."

"I don't think he knows what really happened," agreed Robbie.

I walked to the glass wall and looked out. I heard Paul setting a tray on the table. "I don't know how I would react to what you've experienced," I said.

"Being white, you never will," replied Paul. "Just the fact that you know you won't is a small victory for an aging professor. I need you to indulge me a little longer. I want you to understand my story in a larger context." Paul laughed. "God, I'm using my academia-speak in my own home! Forgive me. Now drink up while I tell a story."

Paul nodded, finished a thought silently, and continued.

"Okay. So I'm in school. I develop a keen interest in biology and sociology. Curiously, one of the professors who taught sociology is a strong advocate for segregation and racial purity. He introduces me to a modernized version of racial purity not realizing I wasn't legally white."

"Eugenics," said Robbie.

"Very good," replied Paul. "Most people have never heard the term, despite the fact that it bent history for the first fifty years of the twentieth century and is still lurking today. As I assume you know, eugenics is junk science based on the belief that the human species can be improved by insuring that only the fit should breed. The U.S. had many proponents of the theory, each of whom wrote prolifically about a supreme white race. By the way, the Nazis read them all and learned from them."

"I believe Virginia's leading advocate was a Dr. Nichols," I said. I watched Paul for a reaction to the name but he simply nodded.

"Obviously, I had a different perspective than my teacher. The subject has fascinated me ever since."

Robbie tried to speak but Paul again stopped her. "I must show you something," he said, standing. "Just bear with me."

We drank our coffees and exchanged puzzled looks. Paul returned a moment later with a book opened in the middle. "Look at this picture."

The picture was a black-and-white print of a family of six standing proudly on a podium. Above them was a banner emblazoned with the words "Kansas State Fair/Fitter Families for Future Firesides."

"That one was taken in 1922. Turn the page and you'll see similar pictures from fairs around the country."

"I don't understand," said Robbie, echoing my thoughts.

"State fairs were put on to show off livestock. Agricultural breeding was a model for eugenics. Folks brought to the fairs for judging pigs, horses, vegetables, and other things they had bred. The eugenicists pushed for judging families like you would livestock. Contestants submitted information about their family history and allowed themselves to be examined by doctors, dentists, psychologists, and eye doctors. The emphasis was on health, but the subtext was eugenics.

"Judges would give each family member a grade that was a measure of their eugenics health. Trophies or medals were awarded the high scorers. These people didn't know what eugenics was. But they understood that better breeding produced better offspring. They wanted the best for their children. The crime of eugenics was that it made all of this racial."

"The gene police," I said, barely aware that I had spoken. Paul and Robbie gave me puzzled looks.

"Sorry. Please continue," I said.

"The message from the eugenic scientists was that Jews, blacks, Asians, and gypsies were inferior to white people. Mix their blood into your family tree and you will have imbeciles, epileptics, and sexual deviants. At the time of the outbreak of World War One, scientists in the U.S., Britain, and Germany asserted that inferior people were breeding faster than smart, creative, and productive white people, and that unless something was done, the human race would devolve back to one of its ape-like ancestors. In the public perception, scientists were god-like beings who never lied, so the assertions had to be true."

Robbie flipped through the pages of the book, staring at photographs of white families wearing medals and looking quite proud. A few minutes later, she tossed the book on to the table. "I've heard enough about the ignorance of the white race. I get it. I don't mean to be insensitive, but I can't fix any of what happened. I'm not trying to diminish the consequences of eugenics, but we're here on behalf of our client who has asked us to locate a child stolen from a hospital in 1953. I believe we have established that you are that person and need to move on to another matter."

Paul regarded her coldly and, for a moment, I thought he was going to ask us to leave. From anyone else, the remark might have seemed a personal rebuke designed to hurt. But what was reflected in Robbie's face was not anger, but sadness. She had overdosed on human cruelty and was trying to defend herself. I was about to say as much to Paul, when he addressed Robbie directly.

"And what new matter are you referring to?"

"Our client would like to meet you and introduce you to your birth mother."

Paul stiffened. "I have come to terms with my skin color and the way it has affected my life. But what I think I've made clear is that I've experienced cruelty at the hands of those who identify themselves as black and those who don't. I was loved by Jennifer Rice for the person I was. After all these years, I don't see the point of meeting someone to whom I only have a biological connection, particularly if there is a chance that my color will be an issue. When my race was revealed to them, I've seen disappointment in the eyes of people I thought were my friends. I don't want to see that look in the eyes of my mother."

Robbie drew in a deep breath and her eyes flooded. Paul left and returned with a box of tissues. "I believe you have the information you came for," he said. "Please use the side door and follow the stones. That will lead you to your car." He took a step, then pivoted. "The people in this country who supported eugenics and the Nazis were never punished. Even the Jews who survived the concentration camps were forgotten right after being liberated. Many died while being watched by Allied soldiers. In time, the idea of a pure race will resurface as something new. History will repeat itself because we refuse to stare it in the face and deal with it. I am one minor victim of this mindset. Focusing on what happened to me and my mother misses the point. I'm sure a reunion between mother and child would make a good story for the Sunday morning news, but I want no part of it. What you must understand is that eugenics wasn't just a quirky part of our history. Eugenics hurt people—lots of people—and not just the 60,000 people who were forcibly sterilized. Germany has come to terms with its Nazi past. Most Americans have never heard of eugenics, and no one is going to inform them. We seem to like living in ignorance. It's not right. It just isn't." He lingered for a moment, took a deep breath, and glared at us. "Please don't come back."

I started at him but Robbie took my arm. "Let him go." She handed me her keys, her hand trembling. "Please take me home."

Robbie turned on the radio, a signal that she didn't want to talk about the interview with Paul or anything else. I had little interest in revisiting the facts or Paul's decision and lost myself in the somber voices of a sax, trumpet, drums, and bass blues quartet.

One of life's big lies is that the truth will set you free. Maybe, but the price is often the loss of the self-generated illusions that allow us to cope with the darkest side of humanity. Historically, the fair-skinned population has always claimed superiority over those of color. Politicians and clergy love to celebrate small victories over this ingrained bias. But the claims of progress serve only to obscure the reality that, as a species, our evolutionary progress is overrated.

An hour had passed when a soft sigh indicated that Robbie had something to share. "I think I behaved badly, and I'm sorry for that. I don't want to talk about it, so please don't. But I think we have satisfied our commitment to Reggie. We found his cousin. We have no evidence that he knew who Abigail Nichols was or had reason to kill her. We know he doesn't want to meet his birth mother. We never agreed to find out who killed Abigail, even if sometimes I said I wanted to. If she was killed because of something she knew, I don't see any way we're going to figure out what that was or who did it. So, I think it's time we level with Reggie and let him make his own decision about what to do next. That may seem harsh, but it's realistic. I look forward to finishing what we were working on before Reggie showed up. That's Reilly's tax problems. Tomorrow, I'd like to go to the county and pitch your idea for the poor farm. Before we go, we can talk to Gloria's sister about you acquiring Gloria's farm. That's what I'd like to do. I want to move on."

Robbie's plan was sensible. As Reggie's attorneys, we had done what we could. But the possibility that a collection of the rich and powerful had conspired to kill Abigail Nichols and was going to get away with it irked me. I couldn't imagine Reggie serving time in prison for what started as an innocuous search for his stolen cousin. If Robbie needed to walk away, that was fine. I wasn't going to.

The person in the middle was Albert Loftus, the man currently accused of killing Abigail Nichols. I might be able to save Reggie, but only if I could convince him to remain silent about what we had learned and how we learned it. I believed I could save Albert, but only if I gave up on saving Reggie.

The reality was that I had never accepted responsibility for saving Albert. Albert would be represented by counsel, and he or she would defend him and ultimately save him. But this rationalization was only true if his counsel cared enough to learn the facts and fight the prosecutor. The prosecutor, with no other suspects, was not going to give up on pinning the crime on Albert if the alternative was a drawn-out, costly investigation that might never find the actual perpetrator. Albert was a pawn in a game of knights and rooks. He didn't have a chance.

The only way of saving both was to find out who killed Abigail. I needed more time, and I needed Reggie to give it to me.

I drove Robbie to Heartwood House, where I had parked my car. She said she'd call me in the morning and drove off. I drove back to the farm, opened a beer, and sat on the porch of the main house.

I called Reggie and patiently answered his questions about what his cousin Paul said and whether I was sure I heard him right. The questions didn't change Paul's message, and the answers didn't satisfy Reggie. I let Reggie vent his disappointment and frustration until he grew weary of the exercise. I made him promise to let me follow a few final leads before he talked to the prosecutor or Detective Hunter. I didn't actually have any leads, but I sounded confident enough that he agreed.

As I stared into the night sky, I realized I'd been in this mental place before. On my path to prison, I routinely entertained the thought that I had reached bottom. The target letter, the interviews, the shock that witnesses were lying, the indictment, and the trial had all been preceded by the notion that the worst was over. Then came the guilty verdict, surrendering for prison, and my first fight with an inmate. Soon, I came to believe that the pit I had dug for myself was bottomless and the worst was always ahead. As hard as I tried, I couldn't help but wonder what Reggie's "small" favor would serve up next.

CHAPTER 15
Monday, February 18

I slept hard and long, though only until dawn. After a long hot shower and a cup of black coffee, I inspected the main house and found that a new crack had formed in the back wall and water was seeping into the basement at a slow but persistent pace. I considered whether it would be safer to just dynamite the old structure, but I still had a few things to remove from the second floor.

Having resisted the impulse to think about Abigail Nichols' murder for as long as I could, I sat at the kitchen table, flipping through the pages of the case file. I was hoping to find something I missed, but the solution to my dilemma wasn't in the file but in facts I didn't have. The key to solving the murder was unraveling the ownership of the Anderson Historical Foundation. I was certain that at least one of them had something to hide—something important enough to commit murder to assure that it stayed hidden. I called Gus and he assured me that he was working on it, but not to expect an answer any time soon.

"How about tomorrow?" I asked.

"How about next month?" he replied.

I was about to head into the office when a small SUV pulled up in front of the bunkhouse. A tall gray-haired woman emerged from the car. She looked vaguely familiar. She introduced herself as Roslyn Hodge, Gloria Strap's sister. She wasn't as pretty as Gloria, but her eyes projected a confidence and fearlessness that Gloria no longer had.

Roslyn studied me for a moment, looked at the main house and bunkhouse, and then rendered a verdict. "I heard stories about you being an odd duck, how you have a lot of money but live like a hermit and get yourself shot and all. And to be honest, I wasn't happy hearing a jailbird was living so close to my sister. But sister Gloria thinks you're the rooster's comb. She talks about you more than anybody. And for that I am powerful grateful." Roslyn's voice cracked slightly, but she remained stoic. "If you want to jabber, you should invite me in."

Roslyn sat at the kitchen table. I held up a coffee cup and she nodded. Hubcap swiped her leg, but she pushed him away. "Never liked these critters. Can't see the use in 'em. They just eat, sleep, and crap." She took her coffee, noticed that two more cats sitting by her chair were staring at her, and issued what I took to be an apology. "I guess you like 'em, so what I think really doesn't matter." Roslyn stared into her coffee cup, her sadness palatable. "Robbie said you wanted to talk about buying Gloria's farm, but she didn't say why."

"I'm thinking about using my inheritance to build a place where folks who need a little help can come and get back on their feet. The facility would be on the old poor farm tract. I'd like to build a house on Gloria's farm where I could live and watch over things."

"Gloria's not ready to move," said Roslyn, "and I don't think too much of having a homeless shelter opening across from her neither."

I sat down across from Roslyn and searched for words that didn't sound unsympathetic. "When I visited last week, she was sitting in the cold, wrapped in a blanket, uncertain who she was. The week before, she knew exactly what was going on, wanted to know why I was checking on her, and wondered if I didn't have something better to do. I stacked some wood for her and, by the time I left, she was asking who I was and if she owed me any money. I don't mind checking in on her, but she shouldn't be alone. I'm not saying that because I want to buy her farm, but because it's true."

Roslyn looked at me again and gave a short laugh. "You are Mary's and Reilly's boy, aren't you? Your mother saw things as they were. She didn't sugarcoat bad news. Reilly never met a needy person he didn't try to help. I suspect with them two voices spinning in your head, you have a tough time figuring out what to do next. But it's not as simple as figuring out what Gloria needs. Our daddy rotted in a state mental institution for ten years. I can't let that happen to my sister. But she can't afford anything better, even if she sells the farm. No. She's got to stay where she is, a place she knows and where she feels comfortable."

"That's my point. She doesn't know where she is. She's afraid to use the generator and shouldn't be trying to light fires in the stove."

Roslyn slammed her fist on the table, spilling her coffee. "She's better off freezing to death in her own home than dying of bed sores in some…" Rosyln tried hard to maintain the air of fearlessness that she arrived with, but the reality of her sister's condition was too much. She covered her face and choked back sobs that threatened to overwhelm her. A moment passed and she stood up. "Thanks for the coffee. The farm's not for sale, but should it be, I'll talk to you first." I walked her to her car and watched as she drove away.

In an email message, Robbie said she had scheduled a meeting with several of the county board members to discuss a development plan for the poor farm at ten and that I should wear a suit. I received a second email that was short and to the point: "Forget the suit. You're not asking for favors. You're offering gifts. Wear jeans and don't shave."

Robbie was in a no-prisoners mood. I wasn't certain whether this was a good strategy from a client point of view, but I shared the sentiment. I had the money and the power to create jobs and revenue. What was missing in her messages was any mention of Abigail or Reggie or Albert. I suspected she hadn't called me on my phone in order to keep me from bringing it up. But I was actually relieved that she had backed away from the case, and I wasn't inclined to draw her back in.

The meeting was at a diner near the end of town—and at 10 AM it was too late for the breakfast crowd and too early for the lunch crowd. We arrived early and watched as the three participants strolled in.

I recognized Pete Carson, a weasely man in his forties and the head of the county board. He had encouraged people to refer to him as "Mayor," a position that didn't exist in the county government but sounded better than supervisor, and he thought of himself as a local celebrity. From what I'd observed, Pete's positions on important matters were determined spontaneously by some personal cost/benefit ratio calculation performed in real-time. I figured he had already investigated the availability of land near the poor farm just on the chance that the project Robbie was pitching could be leveraged to his advantage.

Behind him was a tall, dark-haired woman in a conservative business suit, and a young blonde-headed man with a large wad of gum in his mouth. Robbie and I stood. As instructed, I was wearing jeans and a heavy sweater. The woman was introduced by Pete as Patti Duncan. I was certain that the gum-chewer was named Buzz or Slick, but was mildly surprised when he said his name was Harlow Colvin.

As scripted by Robbie, I was to maintain a sullen, mysterious demeanor. I nodded to each of them but didn't speak.

A young, shapely waitress appeared, her badge identifying her as Celina, and she gave Pete a suspiciously coy smile. "Hi, Mr. Mayor," she said. "Can I get you the usual?"

I will admit that I had a bit of trouble staying in character. The way Celina smirked suggested a broader meaning to the term "usual" than simply biscuits and gravy. Pete flinched, then answered "coffee" without looking directly at her. The rest of us settled on coffee as well and Celina departed.

"So, Shep," said Pete, "Robbie has indicated that you might have plans for developing the farm you inherited from Reilly."

"Before we enter into a discussion of what Shep might be considering," Robbie interrupted, "we need to be sure that what we discuss today will be treated as a hypothetical discussion about procedures and will be kept in strictest confidence. I'm sure we don't want folks hearing rumors and then accusing Shep of misleading them about his intentions."

Celina arrived with cups and a carafe of coffee and another sweet look for the Mayor. Pete nodded. "Of course, Robbie. We're just chatting."

Harlow removed a package from his pocket. "Trying to quit smoking," he said, popping a dark green piece of chewing gum into his mouth.

"I also want assurances that none of you is recording this conversation," continued Robbie.

Patti folded her arms across her chest. "I'm not sure I like your tone," she said. "There's no call for suggesting that we will not respect your request for confidentiality."

"Historically, there is," said Robbie, "but let's move on. As you know, Shep's farm was once the site of a poor farm that housed indigent people. Shep is considering establishing a facility to help families in need. Such a plan would provide construction jobs, teaching and administrative jobs, and support services jobs. We have—"

"I thought we were here to talk about a shopping mall," said Pete.

"Where would these needy families come from?" asked Patti.

"Wherever we find them," I said. Pete started to speak but Patti cut him off. "And how would you be certain that these needy people aren't criminals or drug addicts?"

"We wouldn't," I replied. "I would expect that some will have criminal records and are or have been drug users. The idea is to give them a place to succeed. We will screen candidates to measure motivation, but even the ones we choose will have baggage."

Patti glanced at Pete and Harlow. She clasped her hands together and rested them on the table. "Then the answer is no. Absolutely not. Morgan County and Lyle exist as havens from the troubles of the urban counties. I see no point to inviting their addicts and criminals to come to live here with us. If that's all you wanted to discuss, then as far as I'm concerned, this meeting is over."

"Let's not be hasty," said Pete. "I mean, perhaps we could discuss some kind of arrangement where the farm is developed for a mall, like a theme mall, and the county uses some of the tax revenue to help poor folks within the county. That seems like a win-win to me."

"I'm sorry, Pete, but we aren't interested in a mall," said Robbie. "I think we have enough of them."

"Not one with a Civil War theme," responded Pete enthusiastically.

"A mall flying the Confederate flag might offend a lot of people," said Harlow.

"But it would attract a lot more than it would offend," countered Pete. "And if you have lots of movie theaters and a food court, no one's going to care about the flag. Think about it. I'm sure we could fast-track a plan like that."

The three supervisors departed the diner without further discussion. I took a seat in the booth opposite Robbie and waited for her assessment. She surprised me with a question. "Have you thought about Albert Loftus?"

"I thought we were done with that," I said.

"I am, but I know you're not. What did Reggie say?"

"What you'd expect him to say. Reggie's pissed about Paul not wanting to talk to his birth mother and ready to talk to disclose to the prosecutor in Winchester what we found out. I've again convinced him to give me a little more time."

"To do what?"

"I don't know, okay? I'm working on it."

Robbie looked at me, exhaustion written on her face. "I know you think you can solve this, but you can't. More likely than not, you're going to get yourself into a situation you can't control. I don't want you to do that."

Harlow Colvin appeared next to Robbie. "Do you have a few minutes? I have an idea I'd like to discuss with you."

I slid over and Harlow took a seat.

"I don't know that we've met formally," he said, "but I work as an investigator in the county attorney's office. I've seen you at the bowling alley and heard stories about you and your father. Anyway, I have an alternate idea for your farm. The basic idea is to offer kids who get in trouble with the law an alternative to jail time. I've actually been working with Judge McKenna on a proposal for using county funds for a training facility where kids can learn a trade, get a high school diploma, and engage with the community in a positive way. No one would be sentenced to the facility. Rather, it would be offered as an opportunity for success and not as a punishment. The county doesn't have the funds for the project or the will to build it. So it's just something that the judge and I have kicked around. I know it's not what you had in mind, but maybe it's a way to get started."

"It's not a mall?" I asked.

Harlow laughed. "No. Not a mall."

"You already have a detailed plan for this facility?"

"At the conceptual level," replied Harlow. "Lots of folks think like Patti. People who make mistakes are garbage and need to be kept out of sight. The kids I'm talking about are from Morgan County, so she can't argue we're taking on other people's problems. If you're willing to fund it, I'm pretty sure I can get the votes to approve any zoning changes."

"Well, then," I said, "send the plans to Robbie and we'll look them over."

Harlow locked his eyes on Robbie. "I could bring them to your office, or we could discuss them over lunch."

Robbie glanced at me, then cleared her throat. "Drop the plans by and we'll discuss them after Shep and I have reviewed them."

After Harlow left, Robbie tried to avoid looking at me. "Lunch sounded nice," I said.

"Don't you start. Anyway, I saw you checking out Celina's butt, so you've got no call to be on my case."

"I just said it was nice."

"Back to Abigail's murder. Do you have a plan?" Robbie pointed a finger at me. "And don't tell me it's a work in progress."

"No plan. Not even a work in progress."

We sat silently for a few awkward moments before Robbie said, "I need to focus on something positive. Despite Patti and Pete's reactions, I like the idea of making the farm into a place that can help people. I'd like to walk the farm and see for myself. After that, I can start lobbying other supervisors. We might still win this thing."

We stopped by Robbie's house so she could change into jeans and pick up her boots. On the way to the farm, the conversation focused on the few details we knew about Harlow's idea of a facility for troubled teens. Robbie loved the idea. I was having trouble letting go of my vision of saving whole families. Robbie accused me of having a hero wish, of wanting to save a fictional family from misfortune to earn the gratitude of the planet. The criticism stung a bit, but only because it hit home.

The more she talked, the more aggressive she became, pointing out that helping local kids who deal drugs, hijack cars, and rob liquor stores wouldn't feed my hero fantasy but was certainly more likely to be an obtainable goal. She was still beating this drum and my ego as I navigated the muddy driveway to the farm. She hadn't noticed the old rusty sedan parked in front of the main house or the man with long gray unkempt hair sitting on the hood.

"Stay here," I said, pulling to a stop and bolting from the car. "Can I help you?"

The man pulled a gun from his waistband. He pointed the barrel toward the ground and walked toward me. "The first thing you can do is to keep your hands where I can see them. Get the lady out of the car and don't do anything stupid. I'm not usually violent, but I am paranoid. The gun helps me remain calm and, if you do the same, this will end nicely."

Robbie emerged from the car and joined me.

He looked at us and said, "My name is Willet Nichols. Emma said you were asking about me. Let's talk."

CHAPTER 16
Monday, February 18

Willet Nichols was thin and dirty, his fingernails yellow and jagged. He wore a sweater that hung like old elephant skin from his shoulders and pants gathered in multiple folds at the waist. Leaves and sticks clung to his threadbare clothes suggesting he slept outside at least some of the time.

"Would it be alright if we went into the house?" I asked.

Willet's breathing became uneven and he jerked his head from side to side. "Please. I don't want anything bad to happen. Just keep your hands where I can see them and don't talk to each other unless you're facing me. Do everything real slow like. Sudden movements make me twitchy."

"Okay. My name is Shep. This is Robbie. We are going to walk to the bunkhouse and go inside where it's warm."

"I know who you are," replied Willet angrily. "I'm not stupid. I'm just fucked up. Paranoid delusions and tremors." He nodded as if confirming a thought. "Yeah. I took drugs. Fucked me up good." With his gun, he motioned toward the bunkhouse and Robbie and I turned and walked to the door. As we stepped inside, Willet yelled, "Hands on your head!"

A moment later, the four kitties surrounded his feet. "They won't hurt you," I said.

"I know that. People hurt people. People hurt animals. I prefer the company of cats to any humans I've met." To my surprise, he knelt down and rubbed each cat behind the ears. I considered tackling and disarming him, but I was afraid I might break all his bones.

Willet put the gun down and slid it over to where I was standing. "I don't know if the gun actually works. Anyway, it's not loaded. I can't afford bullets." Willet laughed as one of the cats butted its head into his chin. "These creatures calm me. They tell me something about you. I think I'm okay for the moment."

"Would you like something to eat or drink?" asked Robbie.

"I haven't had scrambled eggs and toast in a while," replied Willet, "or fresh coffee."

"I'm going to go into the kitchen," said Robbie. "I may need to use a knife."

"I'm sorry. I must look a fright and my fluctuating mental state can be unnerving, even to me. If everything remains calm, I'll behave rationally. No need to tell me what you're doing unless I ask or give you a deer-in-the-headlights look. In any case, don't be fooled. I can go batty in an instant."

I left Willet to play with the cats and made coffee, then helped Robbie with the eggs and toast. Willet took a seat at the table. He looked to be starving but ate slowly. With offers of seconds made and politely declined, he sat quietly, his eyes cast down. Lost in thought, he wrapped his shaking hands around his coffee cup but didn't drink. He sighed several times, calming himself. "When I've got something to say, I hear voices, and sometimes it's hard to know which one is mine. I don't see people that often and when I do, all the voices in my head talk at once. I guess they're jealous of real people."

"Take your time," said Robbie.

"I know you're kind people, but I'm not a nice man. I wish I were, but I'm not. Your kindness is, as I'm sure you'll see, misplaced. So the first point I want to make is that I didn't kill my sister, but I probably got her killed."

I started to speak, but Willet waved me off.

"Don't interrupt because I may not be able to gather my thoughts a second time. So, I grew up aware that my father was famous but not knowing exactly what for. I felt entitled by his fame and was arrogant and boorish. Abigail was neither of those things. We were two years apart and as different as children could be. She looked for every opportunity to make the world better. She was comfortable around everyone. She didn't need to badmouth someone to feel better about herself. I envied her self-confidence and courage."

"You said that you got her killed," I said trying to direct the conversation.

Willet hit the side of his head with his fists. "You're jumping ahead! Let me talk, damn it." He took a few breaths. "Sorry, I wasn't speaking to you. Anyway, I know you talked to Emma Forte. Did she tell you about Dorothy Lakeland?"

"Yes, she did," I replied.

Willet's hands started to shake again and his breathing became erratic. He wrapped his arms around his chest and rocked in his chair.

Robbie hurried to him. "Can I get you anything?"

Willet shook his head and grunted a "no" through clenched teeth. "I try not to think about Dorothy. Talking about her is difficult."

"Do something," whispered Robbie.

I left the room and returned with a wand to which a string had been attached to one end. At the end of the string was a clump of feathers. Not too far behind the feathers were Rocky and Atisha in hot pursuit. In an instant, they were on the table, much to Robbie's consternation. But as the felines batted at the toy, Willet's breathing slowed and the shaking subsided. After he picked up the clump of feathers, the kitties took turns batting at it.

"I have to work hard to block out the bad memories or the voices overwhelm me and I can't function. Most of my memories are bad, so I don't think much about the past. When I do, my defenses kick in. Almost like a seizure, I think. The cats helped. Thank you."

Willet took a quick sip of coffee, garnering the strength to unlock what I assumed was a painful memory.

"As I said, I don't like to talk about Dorothy," he said. "She haunts me and, after what I did, she should. My father first brought me to her bed when I was fifteen. She was alive but not conscious. I was told she felt nothing and could hear nothing, but she looked so normal, like she was just asleep. But most importantly, she was naked. I hadn't seen a naked woman other than my mother or my sister except in magazines. My father told me that I had been chosen to help in an experiment that would help keep the white race pure. He told me what to do, but my body already knew. At some level, I knew it was wrong, but we are animals at our core. I wasn't to tell anyone, of course. These sessions, as he called them, went on for a few weeks. Months later, they would start again."

"But what was the point?" asked Robbie.

"My father never said, but I think he wanted to study the color of a baby produced by a black woman and a white man."

Robbie and I glanced at each other but remained silent.

"No one, of course, was monitoring me, observing what the tension between perverse pleasure and guilt were doing to my mental state. I dreamt about Dorothy and prayed that she would die. I imagined that I loved her. I also imagined that she knew what I was doing to her and hated me for it. I thought about killing her, to put us both out of our miseries. But mostly I learned to hate myself and my father."

We reacted again with silence, which prompted Willet to say: "Feel free to make judgments about me. I want to believe it wasn't my fault, but I would be lying if I said I wasn't looking forward to being with her. Anyway, that's not the worst about me."

"You paid for the monument in the graveyard," said Robbie.

Willet nodded. "I did, so I wouldn't forget what I'd done. Of course, I regretted it later when I ran out of money. That's how I am."

"Did Abigail know about Dorothy?" I asked.

Rocky, tired of the toy, jumped off the table, but Atisha flopped over so Willet could scratch her ears.

"Abigail may have learned about Dorothy when she stole Dad's papers, but I need to tell the story sequentially so I don't get confused. Anyway, I was drafted in 1942. Because I spoke German, I was assigned to an intelligence outfit in England. I read reports and intercepts about the concentration camps, but the officers in charge found the stories unreliable. Often, a report of ten thousand bodies was changed to one thousand. A report of a hundred thousand killed or imprisoned was discounted as Jewish propaganda. In 1945, as the war was ending, I was assigned as an investigator to interview Nazi prisoners. That's when I saw Buchenwald."

Willet clasped his hands over his ears. He repeated the work "fuck" several times through clenched teeth. Again he took short, quick breaths, each breath separated by the word "okay."

With a nod, he continued. "GIs were not prepared for what they saw. The emaciated prisoners deserved sympathy and compassion. But to the American soldier, they were repulsive. Skin on bone, eyes bulging, foul smelling, hairless. I tried, but it was too much. I just couldn't grasp the magnitude of what I was looking at. I couldn't look at the survivors of the camp without retching. Who, I thought, could do such a thing to these people?"

Willet closed his eyes as tears streamed down his cheeks. He trembled, resisting the urge to block the memory and enduring the anguish that it caused.

"But the whole thing came into focus when a German SS officer saw my name badge and said he knew of an American doctor named Nichols. He said that Nichols was held in high esteem by the German doctors. He waved his hand over a large pile of corpses. All of this, he said, was facilitated by the teachings of this brilliant man. He asked if I might be related to him. I stared at him without answering. Then he said, 'Yes, yes. His name was Dr. Alton Nichols.'

"That's when I came to understand the consequences of my father's work. The skeletons that walked the wire fence and looked at me were not asking for sympathy, they were blaming me. I don't remember, but I apparently choked the SS officer to death and then fell into a catatonic state. I awoke two months later in a hospital in London. When I arrived at Sweetwater Hospital in late 1945, I was twenty-one years old and psychotic. My father locked me in a room and tried to shock me back to a normal mental state, but any chances for me to have a normal life had ended." Willet shrugged. "Retribution for what I did to Dorothy, I suppose."

He stood up slowly. "I need to lie down. I have an arrhythmia that is treatable, but I'm taking a break from my pills. Might I use your sofa?"

I led Willet to a spare bedroom, where he collapsed on the bed. "Don't go. I may not be able to do this again. Please let me finish."

Robbie arrived with two chairs. Together, we propped Willet up with pillows so he was comfortable.

"I'm a horrible human being and yet you're kind to me," he said to Robbie. "That's how Abigail was."

A deep breath brought a raspy sound from his lungs and a dry coughing fit that I thought might kill him. We offered to let him rest, but he wanted no part of it.

"I was recovering from shock therapy, wandering the halls of the various wards. I was invisible to most of the staff. Those who saw me turned their heads to avoid looking at Dr. Nichols' lunatic son. Anyone heard commenting on my condition was fired. I came to the colored ward and saw my father, a Dr. Marvin Peters, and a nurse examining a baby. To me, the baby looked a little dark, but many do. What I learned later was that the infant was actually a light-skinned Negro. I heard them discussing what to tell the parents about the baby. I was in a perpetual fog from pills and shock treatments, but I knew at once that the baby was going to be killed.

"Then I watched as Emma Forte came and stole it. She saw me but kept on going. I told Abigail what I'd seen. She told me it was just another hallucination, but the thought of that baby being killed unhinged me. I was crying and screaming, behavior that would surely put me into a straight jacket and solitary confinement, when she hugged me and promised she would never let that happen. I didn't see her again for close to ten years. That's when I started to blackmail her."

Whatever empathy I might have had left for Willet Nichols evaporated. Robbie leaned back in her chair, her expression coldly neutral. Willet sensed the change in our demeanors and laughed. "You were hoping for a happy ending, a story in which the black sheep is found to have redeeming qualities. Like most people, I know what the right thing is. But like the vast majority of us, my self-interest trumps whatever impulse I might have to actually do the right thing." He smiled at us and closed his eyes. "Remember that I warned you."

"So you blackmailed Abigail?" I asked, eager to keep Willet talking.

"When dear daddy died, I inherited the house and his money. Abigail wasn't around so I took her share as well. The money lasted until the early sixties, but my drug habit never quit. Soon, I was in debt and behind on taxes. As luck would have it, I came across a travel book written by Jennifer

Rice. Her picture on the back cover drew me in. It looked familiar. It should have, because it was Abigail with dark hair and eye makeup. The giveaway was the words under her photograph. 'When life gets hard, run away and have a better day.' That was what Abigail used to say when Alton and Mom would get into one of their marathon shouting matches.

"I tracked her down and asked her for money. The third time she didn't say yes, and I, being a loving brother, pointed out that there was no statute of limitations on kidnapping. She changed her mind. The money went for drugs, and I eventually lost the house. I lived there even after the county took it over. When Kyle showed up, my old home was fenced off, so I broke into an old house behind where Emma lives. She helps me sometimes. When it's cold, I run an extension cord from her house to power an electric blanket. When it's not so cold, I run a hose to get water for drinking and flushing the toilets. The roof leaks and the place is full of leaves and mouse droppings. I've left it that way to keep Kyle from sniffing around. When I'm not intoxicated, I go to the old homestead to look around. Kyle watches me and sometimes comes over when he's feeling energetic. But I have places to hide, and he just gets tired of looking for me."

"Kyle mentioned that you seemed to be looking for something in particular," said Robbie. "What would that be?"

"The mother lode, the reason that the foundation bought the house and hospital. It's a ledger of some kind. I think it tells who contributed to the Nazis' research programs and how much. My father was a conduit for ideas and money—lots of money. The rich in America were Jew haters, but it isn't fashionable any longer to hate the Chosen People, at least not openly. The children and grandchildren of these well-to-dos are now politicians, judges, CEOs, and lawyers. They take money from Jews and say the right things about them. What Grandmother and Grandfather did during the war would be more than just embarrassing. Fortunes and social positions could be lost. With that ledger, I would be set for life, whatever there is left of it. And of course, there are my father's letters. He wrote the Nazis and other eugenicists. I believe I saw a letter in which the elimination of black babies at other hospitals was discussed. That's potentially another source of income."

"You know that Abigail claimed to have papers she stole from your father? Maybe she had the ledger."

Willet nodded. "She said as much. Funny, she claimed she burned them in your furnace. But I don't think she found the ledger. At least she couldn't remember it. Then I got it in my head that she was lying to me, that she actually hid the letters and the ledger, so I looked for them. Looking became an obsession. What else do I have to do with my time except wait to die?"

"So you want the ledger and the papers to blackmail the people who contributed to the Anderson Historical Foundation?"

"You were hoping for a more noble reason?" scoffed Willet. "Do I think the people who funded the Nazis should pay for the pain and suffering they caused? Should hospitals that allowed doctors to euthanize babies be exposed? I do, absolutely. If I were younger, in good mental health, and wealthy, I would take great pleasure in punishing them. That would be the right thing to do. But I have to answer to my demons. They demand retribution for my sins, and only drugs which cost lots of money can quiet them."

"You said you didn't kill Abigail but caused her death," said Robbie. "What does that mean exactly?"

"I didn't find the ledger, but about five years ago I found a letter addressed to my father from a German thanking him for his assistance. The letter acknowledged the support other prominent Americans provided for research conducted by the Kaiser Wilhelm Institute for Anthropology, Human Genetics and Eugenics. The Institute was run by Dr. Otmar Freiherr von Verschuer, who was a mentor to Joseph Mengele. So I wrote a letter to descendants of the people on the list claiming I had proof that a family member had supported Dr. Mengele during the war. I threatened to expose them unless they publicly acknowledged this support. I regretted sending that letter, so I sent another asking for money. I signed Abigail's name to both letters and asked that the money be left at Dorothy's monument at the church. I actually received a few responses, so I did it again and asked for a lot of money. Shortly after that, the foundation bought the hospital and the house and installed cameras and hired Kyle."

"No one knew that Jennifer Rice was Abigail," I said.

"I hear voices when I'm alone. When I was looking for the ledger a few weeks ago, I heard a voice say Abigail was Jennifer Rice. As you know, the house is wired for audio and video. I forgot about that. I argued with the voice, and Kyle heard me insist that Jennifer Rice was not Abigail. They must have thought she had the ledger because I said she did. Of course, I don't know whether she did or didn't, but that's beside the point. They wanted it, but she couldn't or wouldn't tell them where it was. What I said was recorded. A few days later, Abigail was dead. I think they killed her. Kyle doesn't seem the type, but who knows for sure?"

Willet laughed, the laughter morphing into a cough. "You see where this is going. I am the one person who needed to keep Abigail alive because she provided me the money to feed my addictions. She's gone, and I don't have the ledger or any of my father's other papers. Where am I going to get the money I need to live?" Willet smiled and pointed at me.

"And why would I give you money?" I asked

"Everyone has something to hide," replied Willet. "You came to Sweetwater and asked about the murder of Jennifer Rice. We both know you were looking to find out who killed Abigail. But the police are still calling the murdered woman Jennifer Rice. You haven't shared the truth with them. I know. I called the police before I came here and asked if they had any information about Abigail Nichols. It's curious, yes? Do I have to know the reason? No. I just know that you would like it to stay the way it is. So, you can call the police right now, and I will leave, or you can pay me to keep your secret secret."

I heard a faint "what the fuck" from Robbie and saw the smugness in Willet's eyes. I smirked back at him. "I will happily call the police, if that's what you want. But consider that the police found a cup at the scene with your DNA on it. Do you really want to be a suspect in the murder of a woman you were blackmailing?"

"I don't remember leaving a cup at Abigail's house," snapped Willet. "You're lying."

"I can show you the police file if you like. With your DNA at the scene, you could be arrested and put in jail without bond. The state isn't going to be too concerned about your demons or your addictions. I can't imagine that withdrawal under those circumstances would be very pleasant. So you want to pass your information on to the police? Let me help you."

I took out my phone and asked directory assistance for the number of the police department in Winchester. Deep furrows appeared on Willet's forehead and he started to twitch. I then called Reggie, introduced myself, and said, "I have a gentleman in my office who would like to file an anonymous tip regarding the murder of Jennifer Rice. Please hold for just a second." I offered the phone to Willet, who stared at me, bewildered.

"I'm sorry officer, but apparently the gentleman has changed his mind."

"What the hell's going on, Shep?" asked Reggie.

"Yes. You, too. Sorry to have bothered you. Maybe another time."

Willet slowly rolled from the bed. Neither Robbie nor I offered him assistance. He made his way to the living room, retrieved his gun, and shuffled outside. As he climbed into his car, I grabbed the door. "I'll give you five hundred dollars for the letter you found." My offer was answered by a blank stare. Robbie and I watched him drive away in stunned silence.

Abigail's life had intersected with life at the poor farm for only a few days. During that brief period, events were set in motion that changed lives forever. Abigail became Jennifer Rice. Baby John Mason Langard became Paul Thomas. Harry fell in love with Abigail and took a picture. Doc made a decision he later regretted, sending Baby John and Abigail to live their lives as Paul and Jennifer. Abigail destroyed the documents that might have saved her life. And now, fifty years later, her brother had arrived to ask for money.

As Willet's car disappeared from view, I was keenly aware that events had not fully played out. I just had no idea what was to come next.

Robbie ran into the bunkhouse. When I caught up with her, she had her coat on. "I need to go," she said. "When you're done with Abigail and Willet and the rest of it, I would like to walk the farm with you and talk about the future. But I don't want to hear anything more about this. I'll call you when I get the plans from Harlow and we can discuss them. Until then, do what you have to do."

She was at the front door when I reminded her that I had driven her to the farm and would need to drive her back to town.

"If you're going to talk to me, I'll walk."

The drive back to town was tense and silent. I let Robbie off in front of the office and swung by Heartwood House to see what became of the Residents' review of Abigail's letters to Ruth. I wasn't in the mood to talk about Paul or Abigail, but the Residents sure were. Carrie led me to the kitchen table where we were joined by Harry and Cecil. Frieda arrived and pretended to clean so as not to appear curious about any new developments.

"Tell me about the letters," I said, hoping to avoid a lot of questions. Carrie handed me the letters and glanced at a yellow pad. "Not much to tell. Most of it is personal about who she meets on her travels."

"She likes women," said Cecil.

"That's personal information that we are not to share with Shep!" snapped Carrie.

Carrie returned to her notes. "She talks about Paul a lot. Who's he?"

"Paul is the baby she stole from the hospital," I said.

"So why did a white woman steal a colored baby?" asked Cecil.

"Because she was afraid the baby would be killed because he wasn't black enough."

The answer silenced the Residents, their collective puzzlement conveyed by blank stares and lowered eyebrows. To my surprise, Frieda offered an explanation that was both insightful and simple.

"Some white people think they are better than colored people. A person born to colored parents who's too light can pretend to be white. It's hard for the white folks to know who to hate. That's why they want to kill the babies."

"So Abigail stole the baby to save it?" asked Harry.

"That's right," I replied.

Harry nodded, a slight smile on his lips. "She looked like that kind of lady."

I turned to Carrie. "So what else did you learn from the letters?"

"She says she burned some papers in the furnace at the poor farm. Later, she says she destroyed them thinking the truth would come out anyway but was sad that it hadn't. We couldn't figure out what that meant, but that's what she said. The rest of what she wrote in her letters was about where she was and what she'd seen. I can't imagine visiting Tahiti and India and Africa—all those places."

I was about to leave when Frieda sat down at the table. "You haven't told us who killed Abigail."

"The fact is, I don't know…and I'm not sure I'm going to know."

"What about the man they arrested?" asked Frieda.

"I don't think he killed anyone," I said. "But I'm not sure. Hell, he may have."

"So you will help him?" pressed Frieda.

With all eyes bearing down on me, I said I would and took the letters. I called Reggie from my car. He was not a happy camper.

"It's about fucking time you called me back. What the hell was that about?"

I gave him a short version of Willet's visit—what he said and what he wanted.

"Money? Did he kill his sister for money?"

"Maybe. Probably not. There are a dozen or more investors in the foundation, which owns the hospital, who might have wanted to see Abigail dead."

"Come on, Shep. The reality is that the police won't ever look until they know who the victim really was. Albert Loftus is going to pay for this unless I do something to prevent it."

"Don't give up yet."

"You keep saying that," replied Reggie, "but I don't see what's going to change."

"Come on, Reggie. A few days…"

"Good-bye, Shep."

The call ended and I was no better off for having made it.

CHAPTER 17
Wednesday, February 20

O ver the next two days, I undertook any number of tasks to keep myself from thinking any more about Reggie, Albert, and Abigail. I moved anything I could lift from the main house to the barn. The old dwelling groaned and barked as the foundation slowly but inexorably crumbled. Each loud pop made my heart race and sent me scurrying for the door.

The final blow came on Wednesday morning when the house shook violently and large chunks of the upstairs ceiling fell to the floor. I was on the stairs to the second story when the shaking started, and barely got out the door before a cloud of ancient plaster dust caught up with me. An inspection of the back of the house showed that the rear wall had crumpled into the basement. I called Markus to arrange demolition of what was left. He promised to give me a quote in a week.

The day before, Robbie left me a message that a set of plans for the poor farm was on my desk and that she would be out of town for a few days. She had become non-conversant, an indication that she was stewing over something and wanted to be left alone. Out of town could mean she was in her bed reading, or that she'd gone to visit Eric. I knew better than to inquire.

I made a quick trip to town and picked up the plans. I resisted looking at them, probably because they were Handsome Harlow's idea and because I thought my idea was better. When the main house became too dangerous to enter, I couldn't rationalize procrastinating any longer. I approached

Harlow's plan determined to dislike it and with the mindset of finding reasons to kill it.

The core principle was simple: Find something a kid is good at and likes and train him or her on how to do it well enough to make a living. The facility Harlow envisioned included training facilities for vocational skills—from auto repair to culinary arts—and life management skills. Each resident would be offered remedial courses sufficient to obtain a high school diploma. A recreational facility would be built around a health center that would include vision and dental care. I wanted to dislike it, but I didn't. Begrudgingly, I accepted the plan as far less ambitious than mine and far more likely to succeed. The more I thought about helping kids, the more excited I became.

I spent Wednesday evening looking at a map of the farm. I created scaled icons of buildings and other structures to determine how a campus could be constructed while leaving much of the property in a natural state. All the while, I both hoped for a call from Reggie, and dreaded it when it came.

"Hey, Shep."

"What's happening, Reggie?"

I heard him sigh. "Things got a bit crazy for a while. Detective Hunter wasn't terribly pleased at first, but mostly got over it. I mean, she was glad to find out who the victim actually was and all. She sort of understood why I used the DNA database. And she's inclined to look into what Dr. Nichols and his friends did to minority patients. So all that's good."

"What's going to happen to you?"

"I'm not sure exactly. The prosecutor was pretty pissed about messing up his case against Albert. He had a few things to say about you, but nothing worth repeating. Last I heard, he's going to file charges against me just like you said."

"I'm sorry, Reggie."

"Yeah. But that's not the worst of it. It seems that what we learned didn't convince the prosecutor to let Albert Loftus go. Because there's no way to establish when the DNA found in the kitchen was left behind, neither Paul nor Willet is a viable suspect in the case. Albert was indicted for murder this afternoon. So I guess I confessed for nothing. Probably should have listened to you"

"Are you serious? What about Albert's disability?"

"The neighbor who reported seeing someone coming from the garage was willing to say the person might have been limping."

"Shit."

"You can't help me and you can't help Albert. I know that's hard for you to swallow, but that's the way it is. Besides, you've got other things to think about. Any news about opening up the poor farm?"

I told him about the new plans for the farm and how it seemed like things were moving forward. For a half hour, our conversation seemed perfectly normal. I'd once been in Reggie's place, and knew that his legal situation was no longer for him to determine. And yet he let me talk about a future he was unlikely to share. Then a lapse in the conversation signaled that Reggie was done and he ended the call.

After all I'd learned, Reggie was no better off, and neither was Albert. Reggie had tried to do the right thing, to provide the prosecutor facts that should have steered the investigation of Abigail's murder into a new and correct direction. Instead, the prosecutor reshaped the facts to fit the conclusion that Albert Loftus was the killer. Reggie was to be rewarded for his honesty by being charged with yet unknown crimes. I spent the rest of Wednesday night wondering what I might have done differently. I fell asleep with the case file scattered across the bed. On Thursday morning, I reluctantly accepted that there was nothing more to do. I cleaned up the papers and put them away.

Despite threatening skies, I took the map of the poor farm and walked the property. I imagined an amphitheater for concerts and plays. I found a place for a greenhouse. When I reached the stream that separated my farm from Gloria's, I saw a place where the stream could be dammed to form a small lake that would accommodate canoes and kayaks.

The walk was cathartic and did buoy my spirits. And I might have spent more time imagining the future, but the present caught up with me. My cell phone chirped and, to my surprise, it was Willet.

"I'll give you the letter, but it will cost you a thousand dollars in fifties."

"All right, but in exchange you're going to tell me the truth about what happened the day Abigail died. If I think you're lying, the deal is off."

"Just hurry."

Willet gave me directions to a back road that dead-ended about a half-mile from Sweetwater. He described a path that I could follow to an abandoned home behind Emma's house without being seen by Kyle or his cameras.

My interest in the letter was curious even to me. The names of the contributors were already known. The letter from the German office would help to authenticate the allegations against the contributors, but it wouldn't help Reggie or Albert. And yet I was eager to see the letter and the names of the Nazi sympathizers. I simply couldn't get it out of my head that for all the misery they'd help cause, the reputations of these people had gone untarnished. What I could and would do about it, I wasn't sure. But I wanted the letter. Of that I was certain.

I had no idea what Willet might be up to, but I wasn't taking any chances. Willet had arrived at the farm with a gun that probably didn't work and wasn't loaded. My gun worked fine and my budget allowed for bullets to feed it. I packed it and headed to Sweetwater.

———————

The weather was now suddenly raw and wet. I emerged from my car into a windswept drizzle that my coat and sweater were no match for. I was cold from my feet to my ears, and I still had a half mile slog through mud and the slushy remains of snow entirely hidden from the sun. The cold February wind sent oak leaves into a death rattle, instilling thoughts of loneliness, despair, and danger. I reflexively touched the automatic in my waistband before heading down the path Willet had described.

I had little trouble locating the old house in which Willet had taken up residence. I decided to approach the house from the rear. I found Willet pacing nervously at the front of the house, his eyes focused on the road.

"Hello, Willet," I said.

"Jesus fuck!" he shouted as he darted away from me. "What's with sneaking up on me like that?"

"Let's just say that trustworthiness isn't a quality you're acquainted with."

"You have the money?"

"Maybe I do and maybe I don't. I need to see the letter, and you need to answer a few questions."

"How do I know you won't screw with me?"

"You don't, Willet. But you don't look to be in any condition to set the rules." I partially turned. "I can leave if you want. No? Okay then, first I need you to open your coat and lift your sweater."

Willet complied. "I told you the gun doesn't work"

"Now show me the letter."

Willet reached into his pant pocket and handed me an envelope. "Inside is the letter from a German SS officer thanking my father for his help and for the contributions made by Americans who understood the importance of a purified white race. The letter extends a personal thanks to about fifteen contributors and promises that they will be remembered when the Germans win the war."

I didn't have to read German to discern the names of the American sympathizers.

"Give me the goddamned money!" demanded Willet.

I folded the letter and slipped it into my coat pocket. I removed a stack of fifty dollar bills clipped together and held it up. "The truth will set you free."

"Fuck you! Ask me. Just what do you want to know?"

"Tell me what happened at your sister's house the morning she was killed. And starting with 'I wasn't there' isn't going to make me happy"

"Yeah, I was there. I went to warn her that I had let her identity slip out. I told her about the letter you're holding and about blackmailing people. I asked for money, but she wouldn't give me any"

"Did you see anyone else?"

"No, I didn't. I had to park my car in the school parking lot across the street because of the snow. There were other cars there, but that's all I know."

"You're lying. Tell me."

"I'm not. Abigail was loading the dishwasher when I walked in. I poured a cup of coffee and we argued. Paul could have been there. I can't be sure, because sometimes I hear voices that sound like people I know. So, I may have heard him because he was there, or I may have heard him from inside my head. That's the way it works with me. Abigail once told him I was a homeless person she took care of, so he wouldn't have been surprised to see me. I mean, if he saw me, he might not have been surprised or even interested. Fuck! I don't know. No, he wasn't there. Not there. That's it. So can I have my money?"

"Does Paul know that Jennifer was really Abigail Nichols?"

"She paid me to keep my mouth shut, so I'd say no. She may have told him, but then she was paying me, so probably not. I was high when I got to Abigail's house, and the whole deal is foggy. Okay? I'm not lying." Willet stared at me, pleading with me to believe him. "That's it. Okay? Come on!"

I tossed the packet of bills to Willet. He left without bothering to count it.

I wasn't sure what I'd accomplished other than feeding Willet's habits. I had a letter that was historically interesting but provided no insights into Abigail's murder. Willet had established that his DNA had been left there on the day Abigail was killed. He saw her loading the dishwasher, which suggested that Paul might have been there as well. But while factually interesting, the disclosures were not game changers. A defense attorney might try to use the information to establish reasonable doubt, but Willet's mental state made him an unreliable witness. A reasonable jury would focus on the jewelry Albert had in his car, not on Willet's drug-fogged recollection. More importantly, the prosecutor wasn't going to change his mind about Albert Loftus based on anything Willet said.

Willet had complained of hearing voices, and now I was hearing a few of my own. I had failed to protect my friend and done nothing to prevent an innocent man from being sacrificed to the criminal justice system. I looked in the direction of the old Nichols home and thought about the Anderson Historical Foundation. I wondered what had prompted a group of people to buy the remnants of an old town and hospital and spend so much money watching it. Why didn't they just tear it down? What did Abigail Nichols know that would justify her brutal killing?

Reggie's simple request for favor had drawn me into a quest fraught with murky choices and uncertain outcomes. The choice I was now confronted with was well-defined. While the outcome couldn't be foreseen, the risks could. As the debate continued in my head, it became clear I was fooling myself if I thought I could simply walk away. If I had a choice, I'd made it.

I walked quickly back to my car and headed to Sweetwater.

I entered Sweetwater's Main Street for the second time, not only aware that I was being watched, but glad for it. The recent thaw had removed the charm from the old town. The previous week's sculpted snow drifts were now soggy piles of windblown trash. The sidewalks that once glistened with white were exposed as twisted and cracked slabs of moldy concrete.

I pulled next to Kyle's SUV and stepped into the old sheriff's office. Immediately, I heard an alarm followed by footsteps. Kyle burst through the door to the cellblock, his eyes scanning me for any sign of threatening behavior.

"Hey, Kyle," I said. "I was in the neighborhood and thought I'd stop in and say howdy, maybe get a coffee and cinnamon roll, and see if you can convince me that you didn't kill Abigail Nichols."

"What?"

"Now just to be fully honest, I'm packing a gun in my belt that I'd like to remove without getting shot."

"What the hell are you doing?"

I removed my gun with two fingers, and set it on the bench by the door. "See. Just want to talk, hopefully over something warm. It's really raw out there." Kyle stared at me but didn't move. "Just you and me talking. We can clear this whole thing up and you'll be cleared of any involvement."

"What the fuck is wrong with you? I didn't kill anybody."

"I told the detective in charge of the case that I didn't think you did, but you know how these things get rolling. Anyway, I'm sure I'd be in trouble if she knew I was here, but you were nice to me and I thought I'd give you a heads-up."

"Are you stoned?"

I walked to the cellblock door and opened it. Reluctantly, Kyle stepped in front of me, and I followed him to his living quarters. "I'll have what you served the last time. That will hit the spot. Then we can talk."

I let him stew a bit while I ate and sipped coffee. Finally, I said, "Okay here's the thing. The police accused Albert Loftus of killing Jennifer Rice. That's because they didn't know Jennifer Rice was really Abigail Nichols. You knew, of course. Robbie and I thought we were clever, but you already knew from watching and listening to Willet at his old home. I gotta say, you did a great job of not letting that slip. Anyway, Albert didn't kill anyone, but the investigation was terminated after he was arrested. No one looked at the DNA or other evidence. A slam dunk that Albert did it. But now they know that Jennifer was really Abigail and have reopened the investigation. So they're looking at who may have known Abigail and wanted her dead. You with me?"

Kyle shook his head. "Not really. You sound like you're high or something."

"So, I was talking to Willet…"

"You talked to Willet?"

"Yup. A few days ago and just now. He's got a lot to say, and some of it you can believe. The hard part is picking through the lies and hallucinations. But interestingly, Willet says he disclosed that Jennifer and Abigail were the same people and a few days later, bam! She's dead. But you know that because you heard him."

"Why would I kill…"

"Willet found a letter from an SS member to his father Alton in which the Nazi thanked a lot of prominent Americans who supported the Nazi research projects, a letter which I now have in a safe place. The investors in the foundation are the descendants of the people mentioned in the letter. Now here's the reason you might have killed Abigail. Willet was blackmailing the investors in the foundation but using Abigail's name. So, naturally, one or more of the investors in the foundation thought Abigail was a threat and hired you to snuff her out. You have a history from New Jersey that suggests you weren't the most honest cop, so that's what you have to explain to the detective in charge of the case."

"What do you mean explain? I'm not a hired killer. What's wrong with you?"

"Oh yes. There's one more fact not in your favor. Abigail apparently had other documents that would expose the ancestors of the foundation investors as anti-Semitic, pro-Nazi sympathizers. Willet knew that she'd burned them but you and your friends didn't. So, that's why you—or someone you work for—tried to beat it out of her. Thinking out loud, that might be worth a count against you for conspiracy to commit murder or aiding and abetting. Actually, for a prosecutor, the list of charges seems endless."

"Probably a good time for you to leave," said Kyle standing. He brandished a Taser and motioned to the door.

"I know this is a lot to absorb all at once, but when you think it through, you'll see that I may be able to help you. I don't think you're the killer, but you're the best candidate at the moment. You can help yourself by providing me with the names of all of the foundation stockholders. I'll have that information through another source soon, but if I get it from you, I'll see it as a gesture of good faith."

Kyle motioned again, and I stood, took a last sip of coffee, and headed to the front door. "Be sure to file your report of our chat with your employers and keep a copy in case you're investigated. I'll wait a few days and see what happens before I mention you to the police. Thanks for the snack."

I gathered my gun and left the old jail with no illusions. I had played the only card I had. I'd also thrown out enough bullshit about incriminating documents to be certain Kyle's head was spinning. I was counting on him to share my confused tale with the folks who ran the foundation. Soon, powerful people would be deciding whether the threat of the letter's disclosure would be enough to direct their attention at me.

CHAPTER 18
Thursday, February 21

Having played my final card, there was nothing more for me to do but head back to Lyle and wait. During the drive home, I focused my thoughts on the plan for the poor farm. I needed a survey of the farm that I'd seen in Reilly's office, so I drove directly to Heartwood House. The survey would provide details of the boundary between my farm and Gloria Strap's property.

I told the Residents what I was looking for and we shuffled through filing cabinets full of papers. A half hour later, Cecil raised a file over his head. "Bingo!"

The Residents listened attentively to the plan to build a second-chance center for young adults on the farm. When I was through, I expected to be questioned, but they simply nodded and left the room.

I was studying the survey documents when Frieda stormed into the study. "What did you say to them?"

"I just told them how I was going to put the poor farm to good use. Why?"

"You mean well, Shep," said Frieda, "but sometimes you talk before you think."

"Excuse me?"

"Good intentions don't make up for being insensitive," she added."They're in the kitchen all in a tither."

Sometimes dealing with the four survivors of the poor farm seemed like an exercise in futility. I didn't consider myself insensitive, and I wasn't pleased hearing otherwise from Frieda. "For crying out loud," I said. "Well, then, let's untither them."

I headed to the kitchen where Carrie, Cecil, Jamie, and Harry were sitting around the table. I joined them, but no one looked in my direction.

"Okay," I said, "let's clear this up. What the hell is going on?"

The Residents sat like scolded children, their heads slightly bowed, their hands folded on the table.

"So what am I missing?" I asked.

"We was talking about what happens to you when you build the place for kids," said Cecil.

"It sounded like you would leave the farm and go live somewheres else," said Harry.

Carrie looked at me, her cheeks moist with tears. "We don't want you to leave us." She started sobbing. I took her hand and she pressed my hand against her cheek.

I looked at Frieda for help, but she was busy dealing with her own emotions.

"You are the only person who ever made me feel useful," said Harry.

Jamie handed me a paper on which he scrawled the words, "Being needed is as important as breathing."

Only a few moments actually define our lives. Marrying Annie was supposed to be one of those moments but wasn't. Going to prison was a defining moment for me, given that everything I've since become stems from that event. But looking into the eyes of these forgotten people, seeing what I meant to them and them to me, I had no doubt that this moment would resonate with me until I died. Even my well-practiced defenses could not deflect the sentiment written on their faces.

"Let's get a few things straight. You're my family. I would never do anything intentionally to hurt any of you."

Carrie looked at me, her eyes glistening. "We know that, dear," she said.

"I have no plans to go anywhere," I said, fighting to keep my voice steady. "This is my home. You are my family."

Frieda mopped her eyes with her apron. "You can't stay here, and you know it. We know it. You've got to find a life that's more than talking to cats and hanging out with people twice your age." Jamie handed me another piece of paper. "If you're just waiting for something to happen, it won't."

"You can visit some nice places," said Carrie, "maybe with someone who's pretty and smart. But no matter what Frieda says, we want you to live here. That's our vote."

"If I go through with the project at the farm, I'm not going anywhere. Actually, I'm thinking of buying Gloria Strap's farm and building a house on it."

"You wouldn't actually try and build something yourself?" scoffed Harry.

When I didn't respond immediately, Cecil snapped at Harry. "Just because he couldn't doesn't mean you had to say so."

"I didn't say you couldn't," offered Harry. "At least, I don't think I did. If I did, I'm sorry. Hell, I'm sorry even if I didn't."

"No offense taken, Harry."

"I'm beginning to really like the plan, whatever it is," said a beaming Carrie.

"It's about teaching kids to do something useful," said Cecil.

"I think we could help," added Harry. "I mean, Cecil and I know about building houses. Frieda can cook. Jamie writes stuff, even if I can't understand it. And Carrie paints."

"Well, it appears I have both a plan and a teaching staff." I turned to Carrie. "I don't believe I knew you were a painter."

Carrie gave me a shy look. "I don't think I can teach painting"

"May I see one of your paintings?"

Carrie demurred, but the other residents would have none of it. She finally gave in and led me to a small storage room behind the library. I stepped around an easel and was stunned to see a meadow of wild flowers in bright reds and blues. At one end of the meadow was a meandering stream shrouded in a mist that hid a small herd of white-tail deer. At the other end of the meadow, just visible in the tall flowers, was a puma. The cat wasn't poised for attack but simply watching.

"May I have this painting for my new house?"

Carrie hugged me. "Of course." She pulled back and looked at me, then squeezed me again. "I have lots more."

Frieda announced that she had fresh brownies in the kitchen. What had started as a stressful moment had morphed into a party. The Residents were buzzing about the idea of reopening the poor farm and the parts they could play in its rebirth. Frieda, in a rare show of emotion, took my hand and smiled at me. "You can be so irritating, and then you can do something like this."

We gorged ourselves on brownies, coffee, and possibilities. I was about to leave when Carrie said, "You haven't told us if the letters helped you solve Abigail's murder."

I shook my head. "I'm afraid not. I don't think we'll ever know who killed her."

"Maybe the papers she said she'd burned would help," said Carrie.

"Probably not."

"I'm confused," I replied. "She said she burned them in the coal furnace so…"

Carrie smiled. "Maybe she did, but I don't think so. I never smelled any smoke in the basement, and we all know that when she arrived at the farm, the old coal furnace hadn't been used in years. So, I guess she burned them somewhere else. No biggie."

I imagined a young Abigail Nichols descending the stairs to the dank basement under the main house at the farm. The coal furnace was in the middle. A pile of coal might still have been on the dirt floor nearby. She carried papers and documents that detailed her father's dark side, his obsession with racial purity, and the things he did to achieve it. Burn them, she thought, and perhaps who he was and what he believed could be forgotten. She'd opened the door to the firebox and tossed them in. When the weather turned cold, the furnace would be stoked with coal and the papers would be turned to ash. But Abigail, perhaps distracted by her new role as the kidnapper and protector of Baby John, perhaps because she was hurried by someone coming down the basement stairs, didn't grasp the state of the old furnace. The papers had been entombed but not destroyed.

I smiled at Carrie. "No biggie."

I had a notion to head to the farm, tiptoe into the basement, and look into the old furnace. But the house was too dangerous to enter. If the papers were in the furnace, they would be recovered when the house was torn down.

I went to my office and drew up a contract of sale for Gloria's farm. I called her sister Roslyn and pleaded with her to meet me one more time.

"You can come if you want, but browbeating me won't change the facts. Gloria's not moving and she's not selling. If you have time to waste, that's your business."

I then called Harlow to discuss terms of a contract that would allow the county to operate a youth center while allowing me to own the land and buildings. His phone went right to voicemail. Not to be deterred, I looked up the number of Judge McKenna, the other sponsor of the youth center. The judge had been a friend of Reilly and my mother Mary. Last summer, at the poor farm, I had argued a motion for an injunction to prevent a biological research facility from repossessing a chimpanzee taken from one of its labs. He denied my motion, but he had at least taken the time to hear it. I was certain he would know how to correctly structure the agreement to satisfy the county and me.

He answered on the first ring. "Well, Shep, you're either calling me about my pet project or you're in trouble again. I have time to talk about the first but none for the second. What will it be?"

"Pet project," I replied.

"Meet me at Java Java in fifteen minutes and we'll see what you have to say. I'd like a tall chai tea latte and a slice of lemon torte."

Java Java is a coffee and tea emporium that serves hot and cold beverages, cakes, pastries, and sandwiches. When it opened, most folks thought it was a fad, that people would tire of spending three and four dollars for a few ounces of coffee or tea mixed with milk. But despite the odds, Java Java continues to do well. I arrived first, ordered the judge his tea and cake, and took a seat in a booth by a window.

The judge arrived shortly thereafter. He slipped off his coat and sat across from me. "You're looking better than I thought," he said. "Tell me how you're doing."

"I've been looking at the plans that Harlow—"

The judge raised his hand. "That's not what I asked you."

The judge had a presence that was both comforting and intimidating. His thick white hair and steely blue eyes projected a coldness that likely frightened those who came before him in court. But his objectivity was not without empathy. I took his question as a manifestation of heartfelt concern and found it comforting.

"Better, I guess. Being shot wasn't fun, and getting hooked on pills was embarrassing. But it kind of worked out in the end. Sidney Vail was released from prison, and I managed to send Kikora to a sanctuary for chimpanzees."

"And you'd do it again knowing what you know?"

I laughed. "I guess I'm wired to do dumb things, but yeah, I'd do it again."

The judge sipped his tea. "I'm hearing stories about you and Robbie investigating the murder of a woman in Winchester. Doc says you think it's connected to Dr. Alton Nichols. Is that so?"

I wasn't sure where the conversation was going and was eager to change the subject. "It's a client matter, as I'm sure you can appreciate"

"Jesus. You don't have to go all lawyer on me. It was a yes or no question."

"Yes. That's true."

"I'm sure you have your reasons," he said. "I sincerely hope you'll be more careful than you were last summer."

I suddenly felt the urge to confess that I might have broken my promise even before making it. To my relief, the judge changed the subject.

"I was pleasantly surprised when Harlow indicated that you were interested in my project," he said. "I'm seeing grown men in my court room whom I sentenced as kids. I ask them why they're back to their old ways and you know what they tell me? Because they didn't know how to do anything else. Most of them say they tried to do things right, but I think they were doomed. This project will give at least some of them a chance to get it right. I can walk you through it if you'd like. Then you can think about it and let me know if it interests you."

He sipped his tea and looked at me.

"Actually, your honor, I'm here to talk to you about how we can get started."

A smile spread across the seventy-year-old judge's face, much like a child who has opened a gift and found it to exceed all expectations.

"I would like to retain control of the farm through a charitable entity, but the county would control the operation of the facility. I would pay for construction and maintenance and cover all additional costs to ensure that training exceeds whatever minimums you put in place. Basically, the county would pay the charitable entity what it pays now for juvenile incarceration. Of course, that depends on getting cost estimates and restructuring Reilly's assets as appropriate. And I would need to reach an agreement to buy Gloria Strap's place. My last request is that the facility be referred to officially as Farm Number 38."

"Are you sure about this? I mean, you'd be giving up a large part of your inheritance."

"I'll talk to Gloria's sister about buying her farm," I said, deflecting the question. "Think about how we can structure things legally and make this happen."

"I will, of course. Thank you."

"I know it's time for you to retire. I'd like you to consider being the first manager of the new poor farm. I'd like to help, but I won't interfere with the operation of the facility."

I handed the judge a card with Felix Bauer's number on it. "Reilly made a mess of his taxes. I've been working with Agent Bauer to resolve the matter, but it would help resolve some potential criminal issues if the agent trusted me. If you would inform Agent Bauer that I'm working with you on this project, I think he'd drop the criminal investigation and deal with the tax problems as a civil matter. To be clear, the project can't go forward until I know how the IRS wants to proceed."

The judge ran a hand through his thick white hair. "I've been on the bench for almost thirty-five years, and I've never been at a loss for words.

I can't tell you how excited I am. I just don't know what to say. Of course I'll contact Agent Bauer."

"It's good to finally have a purpose," I said. "I should be thanking you and Harlow. I haven't felt this good since before I went to prison." I laughed. "Actually, I can't remember when I ever felt this good."

———————————

Roslyn lived on Waverly Street on the south side of Main Street. Her home was not just attractive but historically noteworthy. Her grandfather, Charles Hatfield, had ordered the ten-room colonial home from Sears and built it himself in 1918. The Magnolia, as the model was called, was delivered in kit form and included mill work, lumber, lath, shingles, and other components at a cost of $7,000. That was a lot of money back then, but Roslyn's grandfather had secured a contract to supply boots and backpacks to the military and was keen on showing off his wealth to his less prosperous neighbors.

When I was young, Reilly and I would sometimes walk the streets of Lyle and he would tell me stories he'd heard about the people who lived, or once lived, in Lyle. As I stepped onto Rosyln's porch, I was reminded of the story he told about a holiday party that the Hatfields threw after the home was finished. On the back of each invitation was the catalog description of the Magnolia that emphasized its modern features such as central heating, indoor plumbing, and electricity. Sadly, Charles Hatfield didn't do well after the war and invested huge sums of borrowed money in Florida land and stocks. He jumped from a second floor window of his beautiful house, breaking both his legs and one arm. Mysteriously, while recuperating at home with his wife, he suddenly died of what appeared to be a heart attack.

Rosyln met me at the door with a stern look normally reserved for Bible salesmen. She invited me in and pointed to a chair. "Sit and get to saying your piece so I can get to doing my dishes."

I handed her a copy of the contract I had drafted, but she kept her eyes on me. "You don't hear too good"

"The contract calls for Gloria to sell me her farm. In exchange…"

"You're starting to piss me off," she said tossing the contract at me.

"The contract calls for me to pay for Gloria's care at the Bluemont Village facility until she dies." When Roslyn didn't respond, I added, "Of course, if Bluemont isn't acceptable, we can look into another facility."

Roslyn sat in a chair across from me. "Why would you do that?"

"Because I can is one answer. But I guess the real answer is because I want to. I think it works out for both you and Gloria. It works out for the kids I'm trying to help. It works out for me because I can build the music center that Reilly always wanted."

"Bluemont is the best care facility in the state," she said.

I handed her the contract and stood up. "You should probably have a real estate attorney look at the agreement. I'll pay the legal fees. I need to resolve a tax issue left from Reilly's estate before we close, but I don't anticipate that being a problem. Anyway, think about it. Talk to Gloria. Let me know as soon as you can."

The look of relief spread across Roslyn's face and tears streamed down her cheeks. She laughed softly. "Bluemont," she said. "Never in my wildest dreams."

CHAPTER 19
Thursday, February 21

I left Roslyn too tired to feel much of anything. For the first time since leaving prison, I had defined a path for my future. I looked forward to the challenges of building a new "Farm No. 38" and working with Judge McKenna. I was confident that I had solved Reilly's tax problem in a way that would convince Agent Bauer that criminal sanctions weren't appropriate. All that remained between me and the promise of a new life was extricating myself from the investigation of Abigail's murder.

As I turned down my driveway, the sun was setting behind a growing line of clouds. The fading light portended another fight with winter. How that fight would manifest would depend on the ever fickle rain-snow line. To the north, along the Pennsylvania border, the temperature hovered in the low twenties. A hundred miles to the south, the temperature was in the fifties and rising. The local weather guys opted for a forecast that could be defended whether it rained, snowed, or spit frogs.

I was talked out and in need of the special kind of solitude that comes with living in a small cat colony—bathing and purring, but no chit-chat and no obligation to think, decide, or confront. But, the sight of two men stepping out of a black limousine meant that my needs were at least temporarily on hold. The men waited by the limo as I parked and walked toward them.

The driver stood erect, one hand in the pocket of his overcoat, his eyes vigilantly watching me without displaying any concern or fear. The passenger was well groomed, a dark suit visible under his coat. His hands were at his side, his stance suggesting the confidence that came from having money and traveling with a bodyguard.

"Mr. Harrington," said the passenger. "My name is Dr. Marvin Peters. I used to manage the Anderson Historical Foundation. My father was Dr. Peters Sr. who, as you may know, took over after Dr. Nichols died and worked at Sweetwater Hospital up until it closed in the early fifties. Before we get started with questions and to avoid any confusion, my father was a racist and a cruel man. He was guided by his belief in the supremacy of a superior white race as advocated by Dr. Nichols. No amount of apologizing will rectify the damage he caused. So let's start there and see what we have to say to each other."

I pointed to the bodyguard. "So, Marvin, can you ask the Terminator here to take his hand off whatever weapon he has under his coat? I'm tired, not in the mood to assault anyone, and would rather not be shot by accident. And call me Shep. You can call me Mr. Harrington when you decide to threaten me."

Marvin laughed. "You can wait here, Stephen. I'll be fine."

Stephen glared at me. Before getting into the limo and shutting the door, I swore he mouthed the words "I'll be back."

"You live conservatively," said the doctor as he stepped inside the bunkhouse. "Most people who come into money can't seem to wait to get rid of it."

"Conservatively is rich-man speak for a dump," I replied. "May I take your coat? May I offer you something to drink?"

"No, thank you. I prefer to get right to the point"

"And that is?"

"You seem to be operating under the impression that the Anderson Historical Foundation was formed to cover up the sins of our parents and grandparents. You even suggested to Kyle Hooper that we may have killed Abigail Nichols or had her killed. I'm here to set the record straight."

I took a beer from the refrigerator and offered it to Marvin. A smile crept across his face. "What the hell. Thanks." He took off his coat and flipped it over a chair.

"Would you like a glass?"

"No. The bottle's fine." He was looking at a collection of old photographs that covered the café table. "If you don't mind me asking, where were these taken?"

"Here," I said handing him his beer. "This was the bunkhouse of a poor farm. Farm number thirty-eight to be precise."

"I've never heard of such a thing."

"It's another historical footnote, like eugenics and supporting Nazis"

"We don't pick our parents," he said defensively.

I collected the photographs of the poor farm residents, then tossed the crime scene photos of Abigail Nichols' face on to the table where he could see them. "Let's talk about Abigail," I said sitting.

Marvin averted his eyes from the photos. "You don't have to shock me, Mr. Harrington," he said angrily. "I understand she was beaten to death. But I don't believe you have any evidence that would justify your accusations that the foundation somehow conspired to kill her."

I flipped the photos over. "Your foundation was formed almost immediately after a letter was sent to a number of your members threatening to expose their parents as Nazi sympathizers. You purchased a worthless hospital and run-down house and hired an ex-cop to watch it for you. A week after Abigail's identity is revealed by her brother, she's dead. You connect the dots and you have what looks like cause and effect."

Marvin caressed the beer bottle. "I guess you do." He sipped his beer, then focused his eyes on the backs of the photographs in front of him. "One of the great realizations of adulthood is that we don't actually know our parents." He flashed a painful smile. "I certainly didn't. My father and my mother seemed like loving people, like the Cleavers on Leave it to Beaver. I knew my father was an important man, but I didn't know why, nor did I care."

"Abigail Nichols could relate to that," I said.

"I suspect so. Anyway, I bumped into their pasts when I was in high school. When the sixties started, I was thirteen. The public schools were segregated. Some of them closed to avoid integration. I went to private school, so I was indifferent to all that. I didn't know anything about black people or Jews. I started hearing at home about how the Jews and niggers were going to ruin the world. It had probably been said a million times, but I hadn't really listened. My father ranted when Nat King Cole came on the TV or someone with 'stein' in their name was mentioned. To a teenager, that still is just noise. I couldn't see how they were going to ruin anything. Whites and Christians outnumbered them. The last month of my senior year, a teacher asked me about my father. Then he said, 'Tell him a survivor of Dachau says hello.'"

"Did you tell your father?"

Marvin laughed. "I did. I thought he would be happy to hear about the teacher being a survivor. I actually thought they might be friends."

"Shit!" I said. "What happened?"

The amusement disappeared behind the pain of the memory. "He went to the head of the school—a really expensive one—and demanded that they remove the Jewish teacher who spoke to me and all other Jews from the school. They said no, and so he demanded that I leave with him. I refused. He grabbed me, and I pushed him. That's when he hit me. I believe that qualifies as a one of those memorable father-son moments. I stayed in school and talked with the teacher about what had happened to him and about who my father was. I learned from a Jew who had survived a Nazi concentration camp that my father advocated the annihilation of the Jews. Is that irony or just coincidence? I always get them confused."

"What did you think when you received the letter threatening to expose your father?"

"The letter was a shock, obviously. But it was comforting in an odd way. It was a form letter, meaning all of the addressees were identified. I realized that I wasn't alone. I contacted the other recipients. We agreed to form a foundation to preserve the old hospital and home. They knew others with similar family histories, and some of them joined as well. Our goal was to search for any additional historical documents and to ultimately renovate the buildings and create a museum where our family secrets could be revealed to the world. The idea was good, but we underestimated the costs and the will needed to see the plan through."

"So you weren't concerned that Abigail might have other incriminating materials?"

"Just the opposite. When I heard that she was alive, I was planning on approaching her to see if she could help us. But then she was murdered, and I lost that opportunity."

I am admittedly an amateur detective, but one of the first lessons I learned was not to fall in love with a theory that explains the facts. Facts are themselves a creation of the mind. I was convinced that Albert Loftus was innocent, and that somehow an all-powerful Anderson Historical Foundation had arranged the death of Abigail Nichols. But if Marvin was to be believed, this house of cards had collapsed for lack of support. While Marvin seemed as if he was telling the truth, something still didn't add up.

"You said you used to manage the trust. What does that mean?"

"I'm a doctor. What I know about corporations is what my financial advisors tell me. After we purchased the assets in Sweetwater, we were contacted by attorneys representing others interested in purchasing stock. I understood that some descendants wanted to remain anonymous. I didn't think that was unusual. Their money was good and, after all the purchases, we needed it. But the new stockholders voted in a new board, and I was replaced as chairman. After that, any talk about actually restoring the buildings was tabled in favor of more studies and more security."

"So how disappointing was that?"

The look on Marvin's face answered the question. "Extremely."

He picked at the label on the bottle and took a slow, deep breath. "I came here to convince you that the foundation wasn't involved in Abigail's death, but I'm seeing now that I've been trying to convince myself. I'm not so sure what to believe."

"How well do you know the other members of the foundation? My information indicates that some of your donors are hiding behind corporate entities that are pretty opaque."

Marvin laughed. "About as well as I knew my father. I see your point. One or more of them may actually have something to hide. That could explain why they've blocked all of the restoration projects. I'm beginning to feel more than a little naïve. Maybe the word is stupid. It seems I've been paving a path with good intentions, but not seeing where it was going."

"Well, if I had something to hide and the foundation was dedicated to exposing it, I'd certainly pay for the privilege of being kept informed of your every decision."

"So what do we do now?"

The reference to "we" was surprisingly familiar. I had yet to determine whether Marvin and I were on the same side or not. Yet, he seemed sincere, and it wasn't as if I had a lot of time to vet his intentions. The letter from the German SS officer apparently wasn't enticing enough to draw anyone other than Marvin to the farm, and he only wanted to explain why my suspicions of the foundation were misplaced. I wondered if the ledger would be a more powerful inducement for someone to crawl out from behind the protection afforded by the foundation.

"I have reason to believe that the papers Abigail stole from her father are in the basement of the old farmhouse next door. Included in those papers may be a ledger that tells who contributed to the Nazis' research programs and how much. The house is too dangerous to enter, but when it's torn down, I should have access to the place where I believe the documents to be hidden. Report to your investors that I have offered to sell you the papers and the ledger and we'll see what happens."

Marvin finished his beer, then gave me a curious look. "You seem hell bent on finding the person who killed Abigail Nichols," he said, "even to the point of being foolish. You do realize what will happen if someone comes for the ledger?"

I did. I flipped the crime scene photos over so that Abigail's wounds were plainly visible. "No one should die like that," I said. "The man they've charged is innocent. Two wrongs just piss me off twice as much."

Marvin studied the photos for a moment. "Whoever killed her was also pissed off," he said. "I've seen lots of domestic violence beatings in my time. Her injuries show textbook signs of rage."

I grabbed the photos and stared at them.

Marvin gave me a puzzled look. "I'm sorry. Did I say something wrong?"

The notion that Abigail was beaten because her killer thought she knew something had prejudiced my thinking from the moment Reggie had first described the case to me. But rage is personal. Paul Thomas had expressed his anger at the fact that no one involved in the treatment of his mother or of him as a baby would ever be held accountable. The thought of involving Paul in Abigail's murder felt like one more betrayal of my friend Reggie, but I was out of options.

"No, no. You just made me realize something. We're good."

I walked Marvin to his car and thanked Stephen for not shooting me. Marvin agreed to call me if word of the ledger's existence attracted any attention.

When he was gone, I called Paul. To my relief, I was sent to his voicemail. After the answer message and beep, I said, "Paul. This is Shep Harrington. I just wanted to let you know that the police have indicted the prime suspect in Abgail's murder. I also want you to know that the papers she thought she'd burned are actually in the basement of my house. Go figure. Take care and thanks for your assistance." I then called Willet and left him a similar message.

I had baited three more traps in my quest to find Abigail's killer. My hope was that the bait would be taken by one of the investors in the Anderson Historical Foundation or Willet, but not Paul. I simply couldn't bear the thought of failing Reggie again.

———————————

I built a fire but was too restless to enjoy it. Dinner was an overcooked burger that I ate standing up. While eating, I checked my phone and the Internet for messages. I checked my watch as if I had some place to be.

But the reality was that I had done everything I could do. The farm project was in the hands of Judge McKenna. The purchase of Gloria's farm was in the hands of her sister Roslyn. The fate of Albert Loftus would be determined by the importance of a ledger that might not even exist. Until the farmhouse was torn down, I couldn't safely search the old furnace for the ledger.

I busied myself with hooking up the satellite receiver to the television and routing the cables from the old farm house to the bunkhouse. Sleet was falling as I was making the final outside connections. In short order, I had over a hundred channels beaming into the living room. After a few minutes of surfing, I realized that there was nothing on television that I wanted to watch. I settled on a movie where the hero gets shot in the arm and leg and manages to carry a frightened woman while running from a gang of gun-toting bad guys. Somewhere in the middle of a scene, where the hero explains his childhood and exposes his sensitive nature to the woman he saved, I fell asleep.

The movie was still playing when I was pulled from a dream by the ringing of my home phone. I caught it before it went to voicemail, dropped it, then fumbled it once again while picking it up.

"Hello, hello?"

"You okay?" asked Robbie.

"Yeah. Just closed my eyes for a minute. How are you? Where are you?"

"I'm fine. Sorry about not calling, but I've been busy."

"With Eric or Harlow?"

"If I weren't so worried about you, I'd tell you to go fuck yourself"

"Sorry. I'm not myself. Hell, maybe I am myself, so I'm more sorry than before."

"I heard from Harlow that you contacted Judge McKenna and are moving quickly to implement the plan for the second start center. Are you sure that's what you want to do?"

"I am."

"Then I'm happy for you"

"You heard about Reggie?"

The question hung in the air unanswered for a few moments. "Yeah. I keep thinking if I'd been a little more savvy about how things work…"

"Don't go there. We did what we could. Anyway, when you get back, we can talk about the plans for the farm and…"

"I'm not coming back, Shep. I had an interview with a law firm in California and they offered me a job. I'm in San Diego now looking for a place to live."

For a moment, I let the news sink in. "Hey, that's great. You need to do that."

"I can't live in Lyle any more. I worry about you, but it's harder when I see you every day." Robbie's voice cracked, but she maintained control. "I'll be back in a few days to pack my things. We can talk then."

"Sure. That's great news."

Only when I hung up the phone was I aware of the tears streaming down my cheeks.

CHAPTER 20
Sunday, February 24

Two days passed without any hint of outside interest in the ledger. Judge McKenna and I worked through an outline of a structure for the Second Chance Center. I spoke with Gloria and Roslyn about the purchase of Gloria's farm. We signed the contract I'd written with the understanding it was contingent on the county approving the center. I wasn't sure Gloria understood all of the details, but she was pleased I was going to be living on her farm.

The most recent storm had left layers of sleet, wet snow, and freezing rain, making all of the weather forecasters happy. Unfortunately, the precipitation added more weight to the roof of the old farm house, and another portion of it collapsed onto the second floor. Water was seeping into the plaster and parts of the walls, and ceilings had fallen.

I hadn't heard from IRS Agent Bauer about my tax issues since he witnessed the exchange between Reggie and me. Yesterday, I received a voice message from a Nikki Davenport saying she had heard from Bauer, had reworked Reilly's taxes, and had documents I needed to review and sign. She said she would bring them by, but the rest of the message was lost when the power went off. I had no idea when and where to meet her and didn't have her phone number. Agent Bauer didn't answer his phone on the weekend, so there was little to do but hope she'd call back.

Sunday morning started with the promise of sunshine and moderating temperatures. I drove into Lyle for a coffee and roll at Java Java. Once again, spring tried to assert itself. Mounds of shoveled snow and sleet collected runoff water into small ponds that inundated shoes and soaked socks. Even so, the brightening skies were welcomed by a populace weary of winter's grip and apparent refusal to leave a place where it was unwanted.

As the temperature soared toward sixty, my kitties were eager to go outside, but only if I left the door to the bunkhouse open. I finally gave in to this demand. I shut off the heat and rationalized that a good airing out couldn't hurt anything. They busied themselves with bathing in sunbeams and chasing newly hatched bugs while I cleared the gutters of icicles.

Since advertising that I had the ledger, I carried my small automatic with me everywhere. When I spotted a light blue BMW coming slowly down my driveway, I repositioned the weapon in the waistband of my jeans and waited for the car's arrival. I seriously doubted that Willet was in the car, but Paul and one of the shareholders in the Anderson Historical Foundation were still possibilities.

I was surprised when the door opened and the driver who emerged was a tall young woman wearing a baseball cap. She removed her sunglasses and hat, shook her hair free of its bondage, and stared out through bright green eyes. Wearing no makeup, but slightly tan, she reminded me of the kids I played with as a teen, only with more pronounced curves.

"You're hard to find," she said, approaching me.

"That can be an asset depending on who's looking for me," I said.

"Sorry. I'm Nichole Davenport. Your tax attorney. You can call me Nikki."

She glanced at the open front door and the cats waiting on the porch. "Looks like you and your friends are sharing a bad case of cabin fever."

I must have been staring at her, because she awkwardly lifted her briefcase so I could see it. "Can we talk inside?"

"Sorry. Sure. I didn't know I had a tax attorney."

"Agent Bauer said you would be good for my fee and, you know, he can actually hurt you if you don't pay me."

She stared at me for a moment, then laughed. "I'm just kidding. I have some good news so you need to lighten up."

I led her inside and shut the front door. "It may take a few minutes to warm up in here," I said.

"You should open the door and see if your cats have changed their minds," she said. "You know how they are."

I cleared the case file from the café table, but not before Nikki saw a picture of Abigail after she'd been beaten. "Tell me that's official business and not some fetish of yours."

"It's for a client and no, I don't have a thing for dead bodies," I said, opening the door.

All four felines ran in and slowly approached Nikki's outstretched hand. "I can't have cats because my husband is allergic to them," she said. "But I miss them."

I reflexively noted the reference to a husband, then said, "Can I get you something? Coffee, tea? I have cider that I can heat in the microwave."

She responded by looking at my primitive digs and giving me a worried look.

"I'm using bottled water until the well is flushed, so it should be okay"

"Coffee's fine. Black."

When I returned to the table, she was looking at the pictures on the mantel. "Wow. Reilly Heartwood was your father," she said. "My dad loved his music, and I know Felix is nuts about him. He also says you didn't know he was your father until last year. How did that happen?"

"Long or short version?"

"Start long and I'll stop you if I'm bored."

Thirty minutes and a second cup of coffee later, I was talked out. To my surprise, I had told Nikki the whole story of my incarceration, Reilly's murder, how I'd solved it, and at what price. I immediately wished I had been less forthcoming, but the chance to unburden myself was apparently too hard to resist. She had listened without interrupting, her facial expressions relating her reaction to various events in the narrative.

When I was done, she leaned back in her chair and shook her head. "That's a pretty awesome story," she said. "Only you left out the part about inheriting Reilly's estate, this farm, and his tax problems."

"Sounds like a good segue to the reason for your visit."

"I promise you it won't be as interesting as your story, but you'll like the ending."

Over the next hour, Nikki explained her solution to Reilly Heartwood's tax problems. Reilly had not only mishandled his charitable deductions, but he had failed to take other deductions to which he was entitled. By refiling most of the returns over the last seven years, and paying two hundred thousand dollars to the IRS and twenty-five thousand in legal fees, the estate would save over half a million dollars.

"I must remind you that Felix Bauer expressed some concerns about whether you intentionally attempted to defraud the IRS. One of my tasks is to determine whether I believe you are hiding funds or assets."

The warning was delivered with a straight face that quickly morphed into a smirk. "You know I was kidding, right? I mean, I've seen people on welfare who live better than you. He actually told me he was quite impressed with you."

I happily signed all the documents she put in front of me. She agreed to look at my personal taxes and get back to me. With our business completed, she packed up her briefcase. I thought she was ready to leave, when she said, "Felix told me he spoke to a Judge McKenna about opening a facility for kids who get into legal trouble. If it wouldn't be too much trouble, I'd like to see the farm and hear what your plans are."

I went through the conceptual plan that Judge McKenna and I had prepared. Nikki studied it for a few minutes. "I would be more than happy to create a charitable entity that would own the farm and operate the facility in a tax favorable way. Do you have time to give me a tour?"

"Sure," I replied. "You'll need boots because there's still snow in places and lots of mud."

"I have them in my car."

———————————

Nikki was an enthusiastic visitor. She asked about the history of the poor farm, about how I came to play here, about Reilly and my mother, and about the Residents of Heartwood House. The conversation was easy, made more so by warm, spring-like breezes that lifted the still dormant grasses from their icy tombs and twirled them in one direction and then another. At the bank of Lynn Run, I pointed to Gloria's home and explained my plan for purchasing the property and building a proper house there. For a moment, I thought I saw a woman standing at an opening in the gable just below the peak of the roof, but when I looked again, the person was gone.

Nikki glanced at her watch, a sign she considered it time to leave. An offer of lunch in town was politely declined. As we turned away from Lynn Run, a man emerged from the trees. His face was obscured by a hooded sweatshirt, but the gun in his hand was plainly visible. Nikki gave me a puzzled look that insisted I do something. I reached behind my back, but the man in the hoodie raised his weapon, pointed it at Nikki and shouted, "Don't!"

The trap I'd set had been sprung. I knew who killed Abigail. But I had inadvertently put Nikki's life in harm's way and was powerless to save her.

"Let her go, Paul. She doesn't know anything and can't identify you. We can conclude our business before she calls anyone."

He lowered the hood. "Oh, now she's seen me. Too late. Toss your gun to me and let's take a walk."

When I complied, Nikki looked at me with a scowl. "You should have shot him. At least one of us would have lived."

Paul motioned with his gun and walked slowly toward the main house. "I'm sorry about this," I said.

"For now, it's probably better that you don't talk to me"

"She's right," said Paul. "So cut the chatter."

A few minutes later, Nikki glanced at me. "Who is he and what does he want?"

"Paul was stolen from a hospital where many babies born to black parents were killed. Abigail, the woman who brought him here, was the woman in the photograph on my table. She took care of him, raised him, sent him to school, built him a nice house and, in exchange, he beat her to death."

"Shut up," snapped Paul. "That's not how it was."

"Abigail's father, Alton Nichols, was a racist and a Nazi sympathizer. He kept a journal of the names of prominent Americans who supplied him with money. Paul wanted the documents and, when she couldn't produce them, he killed her."

"You make it sound so premeditated. It wasn't like that."

I stopped and turned around. "How was it? How did you come to murder the woman who raised and loved you?"

Paul lifted his gun and pointed at me. His hand was shaking. "She could have exposed them! She could have made the people who did this to me pay for helping the doctors at Sweetwater play God because I wasn't white or black enough! But, no, she chose to protect her father and her family name. Deep down, she was as bad as they were. When she told me she'd destroyed the papers that would expose them, I hit her. I don't remember hitting her after that, but I did. So spare me the lecture on guilt. I'm out of sympathy for humankind. But the world needs to know who they were, and what they did. I want their descendants to be publicly humiliated. I want them to feel shame. I want them to pay with their reputations so people like them can't do it again. I don't trust you or anyone else to do what needs to be done. So give me what I came for and it will be over quickly. Play games, and I'll start shooting," Paul pointed the gun at Nikki. "Who are you?"

"Nikki."

"I'll shoot your lady friend in the knee. I know it hurts, so there's no reason to make me do that."

"I didn't say I had them. I said I knew where they were. Abigail thought she burned them, but she put them in an old coal firebox not realizing that it was no longer in use. The house isn't stable, so we can't recover them until the old house is torn down."

"I'm sure you can see I'm not going to wait, so it's your choice"

"You told him that you had the papers?" whispered Nikki.

I sighed. "Maybe in hindsight it doesn't seem like a good idea, but a few days ago—"

"Move," yelled Paul.

"If you have a plan, say so. Otherwise, I'm going to take my chances that he's not a good shot"

"I have an idea, but…"

"Shut your God damned mouth!" screamed Paul.

I led Nikki and Paul to the porch of the farmhouse.

"Show me the basement," demanded Paul. "If the notebooks are not there, I'll punish Nikki. Play games with me and I'll punish Nikki."

Reluctantly, I pushed open the front door. The house smelled of wet plaster and wood. The air was damp and heavy. The cold penetrated my sweater and made me shiver. With each step, the old house creaked and snapped. I opened the door to the basement stairs. Paul peered down the dark, cavernous stairwell. "Turn on the lights."

"I've shut off the power. I have flashlights in the kitchen." Paul pressed the barrel of his gun to Nikki's head. "No tricks."

At Paul's insistence, we made our way down the stairs one step at a time. As we collected at the bottom of the stairs, encased in a grayness that faded quickly to black, Paul became tense. I considered the possibility that Nikki might be able to run into the shadows while I took on Paul, but he seemed to read my mind. He grabbed Nikki by her hair and pulled her close to him. "Show me the papers," he said.

"This way," I said, directing the beam of my flashlight toward the coal firebox. I lowered my head and moved quickly toward the old boiler. Paul, who was almost as tall as me, charged after me. He hadn't taken two steps before he smacked his head on a low joist.

"Fuck!" he screamed.

Nikki turned and grabbed for his gun. She managed to knock it from his hand just as he swung his flashlight at her head. The beam painted a bright arc in the darkened cellar. I heard her cry out as the light from Paul's flashlight went out. I stepped back and grabbed Nikki's hand, then opened the firebox of the old boiler. The door was heavy and it let out a piercing scream from its rusted hinges. Behind us, Paul was on the floor, frantically searching for his gun. In quick succession, I pressed the release lever on the jack and pushed Nikki toward the firebox. "Get in!" I yelled. Nikki dove into the firebox. I reached the firebox door before the first shot rang out. I used the door to shield myself from the next few rounds while I kicked at the floor jack. A searing pain on the left side of my head dropped me to my knees.

I heard Nikki pleading with me. I heard Paul cursing me. And then I heard a piercing, wailing noise that sounded almost human. The cracking of the massive beams sounded like cannon fire. I pushed hard against the floor and reached the firebox as the weight of two stories collapsed around me. The noise of the debris hitting the iron box was deafening and seemed endless.

And then there was quiet.

I found Nikki's hands and held them. "I'm sorry," I said. "I'm so sorry."

I awoke to a dim light and wondered if my cynical views of heaven and hell had been a bad idea. I don't know how much time passed.

I moved my head and was rewarded with a sharp pain and lightning bolts flying between my eyes. "Shit!"

"It's good to know you're not dead."

"Really? After almost getting you killed, I thought you'd have reason to feel otherwise."

"I didn't say I forgive you, but other than a bump on the head, I'm all in one piece. What about you?"

I directed my fingers to a spot just above my right temple. "I may have stopped one of those bullets with my head, but it can't be too serious or we wouldn't be chatting."

Nikki found my hand and guided it to a rectangular object.

"I can't see it," she said, "but it feels like a cloth-covered box. It's heavy enough to contain a book and a lot more. I gather this was what Paul was trying to get his hands on. Is it important?"

"After all the trouble it's caused, it better be." I moved so that my feet were touching the door to the firebox. "Now all we have to do is get out of here."

"I hope it's soon," said Nikki, "because I have to pee."

I gave the door a kick, my effort rewarded with a sharp pain behind my right eye.

"Move over," said Nikki, "and let me try."

She kicked the door three times before it opened. I moved to the door and peered out into a mosaic of shadow and light. Just in front of the boiler was a tangle of furniture, electrical wires, and splintered wood. I crawled out of the opening and carefully pushed on the debris around me. Nothing moved. Convinced that the wreckage was stable, I helped Nikki extricate herself from the old boiler.

I could see light through the tangled remains of the once proud house. We picked our way upwards and stepped out into the open air through what had been an upstairs window.

As we looked back, dust rose above the remains of the old farmhouse like smoke from a burned-out building. Moments later, I heard sirens in the distance, their urgent screams growing louder with each second.

"I don't understand what just happened," said Nikki, "but I'm sure you'll explain and apologize."

I tried to remain standing, but I couldn't. I slumped to the ground as pain shot through my head. I heard Nikki's voice calling my name. I looked at her, then at the remains of the old house. "I thought I was going to get you killed. That would have pissed off Agent Bauer, I'm sure."

"You are truly one messed-up man," said Nikki, my head propped in her lap.

"That's not an original conclusion," I said.

"I suspect not."

EPILOGUE

I spent the next few weeks in a mental fog that lifted for moments, only to swallow me up again. The bullet fragment that had lodged in my skull caused my vision to blur and my balance to become erratic. The fragment had been removed, but the pain lingered. Having danced with that devil once before, I refused the pain pills I was offered. I'm sure Robbie would have preferred that I'd taken them just to give her a break from my belly aching, but she never spoke about it.

Robbie didn't spare me her thoughts about using myself as bait. In her view, I had acted without consideration to those who cared about me and had endangered the life of an innocent woman, specifically Nikki Davenport. Belatedly, she acknowledged that I had found Abigail Nichols' murderer and had kept Albert Loftus from going to prison. But when I lost my balance and fell on the floor, she reverted to being angry. "You stupid, stupid man."

I understood that I had frightened Robbie, and that the extent of her anger towards me was a measure of affection, but I was relieved when the dizziness passed and my vision returned to normal. The conversation turned to the plans for the poor farm and her new job.

After I was able to care for myself, Robbie headed west to California. We said all the right things about my visiting and maybe traveling somewhere together, but we both knew that none of that would happen. I promised to keep her up to date on the farm project. A long hug and she was gone.

Agent Bauer agreed to accept the amended returns for Reilly's estate that Nikki had prepared. With that accomplished, I purchased Gloria's house and placed the poor farm in a trust. Nikki not only designed the trust but negotiated the deal with the county to establish a juvenile detention center on the farm, which was publicly referred to as The Second Chance Center at Farm 38. By April, an architect had been selected to build the first of the dormitories and classrooms. Construction was anticipated to start in the summer.

The old farmhouse was a crime scene. The excavation of the debris was performed under the supervision of the police. The body of Paul Thomas was photographed, bagged, and sent to Richmond for examination. The box we found contained only letters to and from Dr. Nichols. The ledger, which Nikki had handed to a man claiming to be an FBI agent, was never recovered. Curiously, there was no record of an FBI agent being on the scene at the time we were rescued.

Apparently, Gloria had been looking out at the pasture from a hatch in the gable of her house. "I used to shoot deer from there," she said, "before it became unpopular with the tree huggers. I still like to look. I saw that fella point his gun at you. I thought about shooting him, but if you can't shoot a deer, I wasn't going to take my chances with a human, even if he was up to no good. So I called the cops."

Sheriff Belamy had taken the call but hadn't called the FBI or anyone else. So the content and whereabouts of the ledger remains a mystery.

Both Nikki and I reported Paul Thomas' confession to the murder of Abigail Nichols. The prosecutor dropped the charges against Albert Loftus. In exchange for not prosecuting Reggie, I agreed to say that I was cooperating with the prosecutor's office as part of a sting operation to obtain information about the goings-on at Sweetwater Hospital. The prosecutor received a lot of good press, and Reggie was allowed to retire. I arranged for Reggie to speak with Gus about joining his investigative service, but haven't heard one way or the other.

I turned the letters and other material we found in the box over to Marvin Peters, the former chairman of the board of the Anderson Historical Foundation. About a month after the confrontation with Paul, Gus reported to me on the people and entities that owned the foundation stock. With Nikki's help and Reilly's money, I acquired enough stock that, when combined with the shares owned by Marvin Peters and his friends, allowed us to return control of the foundation to Marvin. I also offered to help fund restoration of the hospital and the Nichols home to be operated as a museum and learning center. While walking the property with Marvin, we found Willet's decomposing body propped against a doorway holding a travel book written by his sister Abigail.

I had planned to find someone to care for Gloria Strap in her house, but a missed step and a broken hip made that impossible. Her sister Roslyn asked that Gloria be taken to Bluemont Village. She made it clear that Gloria would not be coming back and that I could do with the property as I wished.

That Nikki was still speaking to me after our confrontation with Paul was a surprise. I was even more pleasantly surprised when her name came up in a conversation with Agent Bauer about cats. When I remarked that Nikki liked them but that her husband was allergic, Agent Bauer laughed.

"She told you that she was married?"

"Not exactly. She implied it."

"Nikki had a tough time with her first husband, so she's cautious around men she likes. She refers to her ex in the present tense when she wants to avoid any kind of social interaction. I've seen her do it a few times."

"So they're divorced?"

"Well, she's a widow. He came home one night, hit her, tried to rape her, and she hit him with a bottle of wine. He died at the scene. That was five years ago."

"That's rough," I said.

"She likes you," said Agent Bauer. "I don't know why, but she does."

I have seen more of Nikki in the last few weeks. Taxes and charitable trusts are the excuses for her visits, not that I cared about her reasons.

We were walking one day through the pasture by Lynn Run. The sun was bright and the breeze was heavy with the sweet smell of spring. We stopped on the crest of a hill. Below us, yellow and orange wild flowers rocked in the wind while swarms of insects buzzed above them.

"Before I went to prison, I might have stood here and waxed poetically about spring and renewal, about new beginnings. It's appealing to think that each year you have a clean slate on which to write the story of your life. But it isn't reality. Every year about this time, I think that if I could only figure out how I got so screwed up, I could fix it. And every year, I seem to make a bigger mess of it." I glanced at Nikki and laughed. "I almost got you killed on our first date. That has to be a record of sorts. It's a pretty view for sure, but that's all it is."

She stepped in front of me, her eyes focused on mine, a muted smile on her lips.

"What?" I said instinctively.

"Sometimes it might be nice if you didn't say what you were thinking."

"Sorry. I guess that was a mood killer."

She started to speak but sighed away a thought. Then she put her finger across my lips. "I want you to listen without interrupting because I'm going to say this only once. I know who and what I am. I killed my husband, a man who swore to love and protect me. I don't feel guilty about it, but it changed my life. I swore I would never let my guard down again." Nikki shook her head. "But then I met you."

I took a breath but she again shushed me.

"I know who and what you are. I have no illusions that you will ever be a truly happy person. What happened to you has left you angry. You compensate by trying to help others because you can't help yourself. I know your intentions are good, but you should know by now that it won't heal the wound. I understand how broken we are, and yet here I am. I like it here. I like the people in town. What I'm trying to say is that I'm comfortable with you."

I nodded. "Wow. Comfortable."

"Like my favorite sweater."

"And that's good?"

She nodded and put her head on my shoulder. "For me, that's a major step forward."

I slipped my arm around her waist. We gazed silently over the pasture, the warm sun washing our faces. As I felt her pull close to me, I couldn't help but wonder how I was going to keep my past from ruining my future.

ACKNOWLEDGEMENTS

I greatly appreciate the support and assistance I received from Chuck Rieger and other members of the George C. Marshall High School Class of 1966 who took the time to read the galley and offer comments and encouragement.

I would also like to acknowledge my friend, Bill O'Rourke, who always listened to my ideas and helped me filter the good from the bad. I miss him greatly.

It is almost a cliché for writers to thank their spouses. Cliché or not, Sonya has read drafts that should never have been printed. She has also endured the moods of her author-husband with a patience and an unwavering objectivity that have made me a better writer. As she often notes, "we're a team." Yes, that and more.

ABOUT THE AUTHOR

I am a retired patent attorney living in Florida with my wife, Sonya, and our feline, Tsuki. I spent most of my life in the Washington, D.C. area, growing up in McLean, Virginia before the beltway was constructed. Several of my grade school classmates lived on nearby farms, and McLean had a small-town feel to it. Gossip spread without the Internet. Party lines were common. Secrets were hard to keep.

When I was in my early thirties, my life pivoted when I was accused of a crime I didn't commit. My defense counsel and I discussed plans for my likely indictment and possible imprisonment. I expected to be handcuffed and paraded in front of the media. This experience with the so called justice system ended after a two-year ordeal, without an indictment and without going to trial. Even so, it could have ended differently.

Sadly, I will never fully believe that prosecutors, investigators, or the government are as interested in the truth as they are in getting a conviction, an attitude that I share with the semi-fictional Shep Harrington.